Y0-BEM-730

Timeline Books ™

Also by Matthew Bayan:

EAT FAT BE HEALTHY: When A Low-Fat Diet Can Kill You

The Firecracker King

Matthew Bayan

The Firecracker King

Copyright © 2012 by Matthew Bayan

All rights reserved. No part of this book may be reproduced in any form or by any electronic or mechanical means, including information storage and retrieval systems, without permission in writing from the publisher, except by a reviewer who may quote brief passages in a review.

The Timeline Books name and logo are trademarks of Timeline Books.

First Edition - March 15, 2012

The characters and events in this book are fictitious. Any similarity to real persons, living or dead, is coincidental and not intended by the author.

ISBN-13: 978-0615616360
ISBN-10: 0615616364

CHAPTER 1
July 1, 1965

Only three days to the Fourth of July, the holy of holies for a firebug like me. Time slowed to a fat waddle. The air itself felt lush and thick. Food tasted better.

My best friend, Eddie Sparrow, showed up after dinner with a fishing pole across his shoulder. "Jake, let's take out *Crater Face*," he said. "I got a new bass lure." Eddie's crusade this summer was to catch a bass. He'd never caught one, but that just gave him a reason to buy more lures. Eddie could afford new lures, and reels, and fishing poles. Me? I had one spinner lure that had to serve for catching everything.

My family clung to the lowest rung of the economic ladder that could still be considered middle class. Hell, we had spaghetti four times a week. But I never felt down and out; I had something better than all the lures and model planes and crap that Eddie might ever buy. I had the best back yard in the world: Granger Lake. It stretched a mile long and a half mile across. A sandy beach, an old dock, and a dinged-up aluminum rowboat made me feel like a prince.

As shadows fanned out from the ancient oaks over the lily pads and algae-green water, we pushed *Crater Face* away from my dock. *Crater Face* was the most god-awful rowboat on the lake. Dinged and banged and once used for target practice, its twelve-foot aluminum hull looked like the surface of the moon. Nine bullet holes required daily stuffing with bubble gum.

Eddie rowed after tying his fishing pole to the rear seat and playing out line over the stern. I flicked my spinner lure out as well. Turning around and dropping onto the bottom of the boat, I leaned back against the stern with my feet draped across the rear seat, facing Eddie instead of our wake. My pole extended back over my shoulder.

Eddie said, "You *really* look like your lazy ass is fishin'," as he pushed a lock of sun-bleached hair off his forehead. The freckles across his cheekbones had spread and soon would merge into the splotchy mass he called his "summer face." Except for the freckles, Eddie and I looked like brothers. Two fourteen-year-old, brown-eyed bean poles.

"Hey, I need to relax," I said.

"Whasamatta, gettin' old? Need a freakin' nap?"

"Eat shit and die."

"Bite me."

We trolled and bickered as the sky burnt to copper and crickets on shore began their nightly madness. The oarlocks creaked a steady rhythm, the breeze died, and the lake surface became a mirror reflecting the darkening sky. In this brief time between day and night, the lake seemed to hold its breath. Bullfrogs barked from the shallows and charcoal-colored chimney swifts twittered and skimmed so close to the water sometimes their wings rippled the surface.

"Better head back. Gettin' hungry," Eddie said.

"You're always hungry. You should weigh two tons with all you eat."

"All this damn rowin' burns it up. How 'bout on the way back you take one oar, I'll take the other? We'll go like hell."

"It's my boat. You want to fish in my boat, you have to row."

"One of these days I'm gonna mutiny."

"Then I'll hang you from the yardarm."

"You don't even have a yardarm. This is a freakin' rowboat."

"Picky, picky."

Eddie quickened the pace. "Pull in your lure. You can't troll at the speeds we're gonna hit."

Before I could move, my fishing rod bent back and jerked out of my grasp. I spun and grabbed at the base of the pole and barely caught it before it went overboard. "Stop, Eddie. Back up, back up!"

Line zipped out of my reel. Eddie dug the oars deep to bring us to a stop, then propelled the boat backwards. "Slow down," I said. My line was almost vertical in the darkening water.

"What is it?" he said.

"Feels like a snag."

"Way out here? Too deep for a freakin' snag."

I reeled in slowly, not wanting the line to break, fighting the dead weight of whatever my lure had hooked.

"Aw, hell, Jake, just cut the damn line."

"No way. That's my only lure."

"I'll give you another one."

Something several feet down brightened as it rose. A clump of white cloth broke the surface.

"Looks like a dress," I said.

"Somebody was skinny-dippin' again. How you think she got home without a dress? How come we're never here when these naked babes are runnin' around?"

"One look at your freckle-face and they'd run so fast you wouldn't see anything anyway."

"Okay, Zit-Man." Eddie had to have the last word.

I held my fishing pole in my right hand and grabbed the cloth with my left, but as I tugged, the cloth would not come out of the water. I set down my fishing pole and clutched the cloth with both hands. Even a slight pull told me it wasn't coming up easily. As I tried for a better hold, my hands closed on something inside the cloth. Something rubbery.

"Are we ever goin' home?"

"Dammit, Eddie, stop bitching and help me with this."

"Help you what? Just yank the damn lure out already."

"I need to pull it onboard."

"What for? See if she left her underwear too? You're sick, Jake, but I like the way you think."

"Give me a hand."

"You can't lift a freakin' dress? Crap." Eddie made a fuss about stepping over the rear seat as I centered the cloth at the stern so we wouldn't tip over when we pulled.

White cloth. Red polka dots. It didn't look like much. We weren't the strongest guys on earth, but we still should have had the power to lift a wet dress. We could get it only a few inches above the surface.

Eddie lost his smirk and glanced at me. "This isn't just a dress."

My grip slipped and the dress turned and just under the surface of the water something moved. A pale hand waved back and forth then sunk out of sight. My head snapped to face Eddie.

7

"What?" he said.

Looking at me, he hadn't seen it. My heart crashed around inside my chest. Before I could think about it I tightened my grip and spread my feet.

"Eddie, one, two, three." Eddie and I yanked on the cloth. A face rose from the water. Empty eye sockets stared at us. What was left of the lips hung in blue tatters down her chin. A strand of black hair streamed across a cheek paler than my grandmother's china.

Screaming, I jumped back, tripping over the rear seat and sprawling into the bottom of the rowboat. The aluminum boomed with the impact. Eddie's panic erupted a half-second after mine and his scream did not stop until we found ourselves in the bow of the boat, holding onto the sides as if a hurricane blasted us.

"What are we gonna do? What are we gonna do?" Eddie's voice rose two octaves.

It felt like the world stopped spinning on its axis. We stared at each other. Eddie's face pulled into a grimace that looked like it would crack his cheeks. An electric green dragonfly landed on the tip of the bow and stared at us as we stared at each other. Nothing moved. Anywhere.

Then we heard a tiny click. It could have been a gunshot for the effect it had on us. Our heads snapped around to the source of the sound.

Click.

My reel rotated and clicked again. Then again and again as the body settled back into the water and the line played out.

I instinctively reached for my fishing rod. Eddie shouted, "Throw it in, just throw it in. Let's get the hell out of here!"

"We can't just leave her here."

"Yes we can!" Eddie jumped onto the middle seat and grabbed the oars. He heaved and the boat lurched. My reel clicked madly as the line spun out. Eddie heaved again and the boat picked up speed.

"Eddie, no."

Eddie didn't listen. In seconds, he forced the boat to top speed.

My reel spun like crazy. The line would soon run out. Reaching into my tackle box I grabbed a red and white bobber, stretched out to the tip of my fishing rod past the guide ring, and clicked the bobber onto the line just as the last of it flew out of my reel.

The tiny bobber diminished quickly to a dot and disappeared in the gathering gloom.

CHAPTER 2
Two Hours Later

"Turtles got to the face. Holy Christmas, look at that mess." A township cop in rubber hip boots waded into the shallows and steadied the search boat as the crew pulled the body out of it onto the low, wooden dock.

"Hasn't been down long or she'd have a lot more damage," one of them said.

"Whaddaya think?"

"Day or two maybe."

I sat in a power boat with two township cops, wishing Eddie was there. The police had not been able to get Eddie back to the lake. He was practically incoherent.

Though the police had come ready with divers and grappling hooks, they didn't need any of that stuff. Even though it was well past sunset, I led them right to my bobber. Police boats closed in and lit up the place brighter than noon. Tugging gingerly on the fishing line, so it wouldn't snap, they drifted to a spot right above the body. Just as I had done hours before, they slowly pulled the line until the corpse surfaced. Before the body came out of the water, they hustled me out of there.

On the dock, her flesh glowed in the spotlights. It looked like she had a black spiderweb tattooed to her face, but it was just her long hair scattered randomly across her upper torso. When they lifted her onto a body bag, her limbs flopped rubber-like against the wood decking and sent dull thumps through the dock. That was the creepiest thing I've ever heard. That's when it hit me that she was really dead. They zipped the black bag shut and three cops hauled it up the embankment to where a circus of blinking lights lit up the trees.

The two officers kept our search boat ten feet from the dock. No talking. Just eyeballing me. The bigger one, Tony Rubino, was built like a fireplug with the face of an ape. He and I had a long history. He hated my guts. I hated his guts. One of life's simpler relationships.

"Do I get to sit out here all night?" I said, slapping my head as the millionth mosquito tried to drill me. My bug repellant weakened with each bead of sweat that rolled off me.

Mosquito squadrons swarmed overhead, watching, waiting, occasionally sending a scout to see if it was safe yet. New Jersey mosquitoes are so big they can carry off small children. They must be mutants. They actually *like* DDT; it makes them stronger.

The cops ogled me like I was a freak show. Two-headed Boy. Beast Child. The Incredible Infinite Asshole.

Rubino growled, "How'd you know to look in that spot?"

"What spot? There was no spot."

"You know her?"

"I have no idea who she is."

"You and your friend fish back there often?"

"I go by myself most of the time."

"You see anybody else back there?"

"No."

"Just you, huh?" Rubino's sunken eyes fixed on me like I was dessert.

Oh, great.

"If you think I had something to do with this, you're more nuts than I thought." I wouldn't dare talk to other cops like this, but with Rubino, I didn't care. I wanted him to punch me. It would be worth it to get him thrown off the force.

"It's a big lake, but you knew just where to find the body. Some coincidence." Rubino's black eyes squinted and his slug lips pulled back from those yellow things he called teeth. He didn't need to hit me. He was a happy man. His eyes roved back and forth in their sockets as if he was measuring me for a prison jump suit.

"You've been in trouble before," the little cop muscled in. He had a face like a squirrel and skin like cream cheese. Probably never worked the day shift.

"Uh, yeah, officer. Big trouble. I raced a go-cart on a public street. Let's see, I raised about a million flies and let them loose in the school cafeteria. I'm a dangerous go-carting, fly-raising criminal. You better take me away."

Yeah, my mouth is not always under my control.

Rubino said, "What about the explosion?"

"What explosion?"

"You know damn right well what explosion, you little pyromaniac. The dumpster behind the supermarket."

Oh, this was Rubino's big move? A Perry Mason smile spread across his face as if he had just tripped me up, caught me by surprise. "Well, I think I can tell you how that happened," I said.

"Okay, Professor Smartass, how did it happen?" He looked like a wolverine about to feed on a rabbit.

I cleared my throat and raised my left index finger, imitating paintings I'd seen of Socrates. "Clearly, it was spontaneous combustion of the methane caused by decay of foodstuffs and other organic waste material. Any fifth grader would know that."

Rubino's lips squirmed like worms on a hot sidewalk.

Squirrel-face just eyeballed me harder.

CHAPTER 3
July 2, 1965

When my parents picked me up from the police station last night, the police told us not to talk about what happened until they identified the girl's body.

Fine with me. July 4th rushed toward us and every boy in the neighborhood was losing his mind. I was the worst. As June progressed, I changed into a werewolf, suffering through the day, pining for the moon. Being a firebug is a terrible disease. By noon, I had almost forgotten about yesterday's adventure.

I had this Uncle Frank who knew someone who knew someone. I never asked who the someones were. In New Jersey you learned the rules of conduct at an early age.

If I gave Uncle Frank money in early May, by the time school was out I had a trunkful of fireworks. I mean I had everything: long strings of firecrackers, boxes of cherry bombs and tankers, aerial bombs, Roman candles, smoke bombs, rockets.

We measured explosives against a standard: what could something do to some neighbor's mailbox? Regular firecrackers had no effect on a mailbox. They rarely even made the door fly open.

Cherry bombs reigned as my favorite. Perfect for throwing, bright red, with a green fuse, they looked like the fattest cherries ever grown. A cherry bomb would blow the door right off a mailbox and leave the mailbox bulged out of shape.

At the top of the power pyramid stood tankers, also known as M-80s. These little cardboard cylinders packed more power than cherry bombs, but you couldn't throw them as far because of their shape. Properly placed, a tanker could shred a mailbox.

For the month of June, I ruled the neighborhood. My father called me the Firecracker King. How much for issue #1 of *The Fantastic Four*? Ten packs of firecrackers. Mickey Mantle's rookie baseball card? Fifty cherry bombs. Fireworks functioned far better than money. Offer a guy money for something he didn't want to sell and he might yawn. Offer him a three-foot rocket with a quarter stick of

15

dynamite in the nose and you had his attention.

I knew how gangsters felt with their secret deals. I had power. Status.

Sometimes I wanted something so badly, I didn't care what I traded. Like today. For the past week I'd been hounding my other best friend, Steve Lezar, to see the 45 RPM records his sister gave him when she got married and moved out. With the Fourth of July looming, Steve needed fireworks, but he was flat broke. Opportunity.

"Here they are," Steve said, as we got to the bottom of his basement stairway. Three wooden milk crates of 45s sat along a cinder block wall.

I had music stamped into my guts like a watermark on a bank check, but during the first years of rock and roll and Doo-Wop, I was too young to go to a music store and buy records. By the time I had money and was old enough to go downtown by myself, the classic era was over. If I could even find these old records in a store bin, they cost a dollar or more. A dollar bought eight comic books and four red twizzlers. Entertainment presented harsh choices.

So, I had to scrounge through people's basements to find ten-year-old records that were usually scratched so badly that when I played them it sounded like someone was sending radio signals from Jupiter.

As I pored through Steve's crates, I thought I would faint. I had never seen such pristine records: mirror surfaces, no scratches, and even the paper sleeves were unwrinkled. As cool as it was in his basement, I broke a sweat. The Five Satins, The Paragons, The Duprees, Bill Haley and The Comets, Buddy Holly, Elvis on Sun Records, Little Richard.

I'd kill for these records. The problem was that Steve and I had been friends since first grade. Damn, I hated doing business with friends.

I tried disinterest. "Maybe I could pick through and just take what I want."

"No picking through. All three or nothing." Steve said it matter-of-factly as he settled onto the concrete floor next to the crates and crossed his legs. His hazel eyes crinkled at the corners. I'd seen that look in a hundred customers. He had an ace up his sleeve.

"So, what do you want?"

He crossed his meaty arms across his chest. "Five gross of cherry bombs."

"You crazy? That's over seven hundred. You'll wind up in the hospital. For your own good, I can't give you that much. Two gross."

"Eddie said he'd give me five."

Ah, Eddie was the ace. "Did you actually see Eddie's cherry bombs?"

Steve looked away for a second.

I pounced. "You didn't see his cherry bombs, because he doesn't have any. He was at my house a few days ago trying to buy - let me see - what was it? Oh, yeah, he wanted five gross of cherry bombs. Problem was, he didn't have enough money and I don't do credit."

Steve ran his left hand back and forth across his blond buzz-cut, like he wanted to build up a static charge to spark his brain to life. "Let me think about it."

"Think about it? Steve, what's your Fourth of July gonna be like? You and Eddie and his little sister waving sparklers?"

Wrinkles creased Steve's wide forehead. I pressed on. "You don't accept my offer, I'll never sell you another goddamn thing."

Steve rolled back on his haunches on the dusty basement floor. Legs crossed, stomach bulging, he looked like the Buddha. "I thought we were friends." His face scrunched into a pout.

"Yeah, me too, but you're pissin' in my pocket here. I mean, five gross of cherry bombs? C'mon, man, maybe you want my left nut too?"

Then I saw the danger I was in. Eddie had more crazy crap than a junk shop. He could sell stuff and raise enough money. If I refused to sell cherry bombs to him, he could go downtown and find another source. Eddie would find a way to get Steve's records. Haggling with Eddie for the records would become a nightmare that could go on for months. Eddie made used car dealers look ethical. I could wind up a pauper. Or I could swallow my pride and make this deal happen now.

"Steve, you're right, we're friends. So, here's my best offer. Four gross. More than you've ever had in your life."

That hand scruffed across his crewcut again. It came down to who was more desperate. I nudged. "Steve, what if Eddie can't scrounge enough money? Can you take that chance? The Fourth is only two days away."

He finally stopped rubbing his head and said, "I'll make the deal on one condition."

"Oh, Jeez." I rolled my eyes. Here we go. Extra innings.

"Tell me about the body."

"I can't. Promised the cops I wouldn't. Ask Eddie."

"I already did. He won't talk about it. He's totally messed up."

"He's a weenie."

"You want these records?" Steve said.

Sometimes you have to bend with the wind. "I'll tell you *after* we move these records to my house."

"You don't trust me?"

"I don't trust Eddie."

I practically teleported those crates to my house.

CHAPTER 4
July 3, 1965
The Next Day

Summer gave me all the time in the world to read. Not the crap they gave us in school, but good stuff like Heinlein, Sturgeon, and Bradbury. I'm glad libraries are free. If I had to pay for the masses of books I devoured, I'd be broke.

I rolled onto my stomach on the thick bluegrass that carpeted the hill at the back of my house. A red maple jutted out over the sand and part way over the water. I lolled away my mornings in this shady spot, waiting for the sun to heat the surface of the lake.

After finding a body, I thought I should feel much more crummy than I did. Not that I felt great. Last night I dreamed of that doll face and those holes where there should have been eyes. I needed to immerse myself in someone else's world today and wipe those images from my mind.

I read my book while my left hand absently scratched the battle-singe a Roman candle ball had left on the top of my head earlier in the week.

"Whatcha readin'?"

Out of nowhere, like a ghost whispered in my ear. I couldn't have spun off my stomach any faster if I'd been zapped with a cattle prod. A silhouette stood above me, framed by blinding sunlight. I swiveled sideways into the shade and squinted.

When I recognized the figure looming over me, my heart tripped into overdrive. My tongue had a stroke.

"I'm Sharon," she said.

As if she needed to tell me. Every school-age male within a hundred miles of Trenton knew of Sharon Young. Maybe every guy in New Jersey. And now she stood on my beach, talking to *me*. Me, a fourteen-year-old nobody with skinny arms and a stupid crewcut. The most whispered-about, most dreamed-about girl in high school stripped off her T-shirt. I prepared for the heart attack.

I wished I had a camera as she wriggled out of her cut-off jeans. Nobody would ever believe that a dork like me could have this happen.

19

My lungs felt like all the air in the world was rushing into outer space as I gasped to catch my breath. What a sad twist of fate if I fainted in the middle of this historic event.

To get the sun out of my eyes, I scuttled farther under the maple, gaping at this golden-skinned statue of muscle and curves, barely held in by a silky white bikini. A French bikini.

A year after *The Girl in the Bikini* pranced Brigitte Bardot across a million movie screens, a few of the more daring girls showed up at local beaches with the parent-approved two-piece bathing suit in denim and plaid. These pale copies of the real thing showed maybe two inches of midriff with none of that anywhere near a navel.

Not Sharon. This white wisp of fabric definitely did not have the parental seal of approval. Her navel drifted on a sea of skin with the nearest shore far to the south. It looked like spiders had spun this silky creation right onto her body. I envied those spiders.

She settled cross-legged on the grass facing me. "You're Jake, aren't you?"

I nodded. I couldn't manage much more response as I fought hard just to stay conscious.

"You have the nicest beach on this side of the lake."

You have the nicest body on this side of the planet. Yeah, great compliment, Jake. Why don't you try that one? My brain derailed. Could the grin I had plastered across my face look any more stupid? If I didn't say something soon, she'd think I was a retard.

"I usually swim off the point." She waved in the general direction of a promontory a couple hundred yards away. "But I saw a snake in the weeds. Mind if I swim here?"

The gap between me and being cool was the size of the Grand Canyon, but I tried. I forced my crippled tongue to move. "S-sure. Anytime." Yeah, like she would now just drop in whenever she felt like it. Maybe I *was* retarded to dream that this could happen more than once.

"You been in yet? How's the water?" She glanced over her shoulder into the shimmer of morning sun off the lake.

In those seconds when her eyes looked away, my own eager orbs raked over her body, cataloguing every microscopic detail. The golden down on her arms. The tanned texture of her skin. How much her bikini top held in and how much it didn't. How the strings of her bikini bottom pulled against the tight muscles in her hips. My friends would quiz me mercilessly on these things later and my level of detail would earn me either reverence or ridicule.

She caught me staring between her legs. I couldn't help it. I had never seen a woman's pubic hair, at least not right in front of me. Hers peeked around the edges of the sheer material like bronze coils.

Without the slightest embarrassment, she reached down and tucked the stray hairs into her suit. "I probably should shave for summer."

Shave? Did women do such things down there? It was a region of complete mystery.

As her golden eyes focused on me, I realized how different she was from all the other good-looking girls. She never wore make-up. In school, she wore simple dresses. During summer vacation, I had never seen her in anything but cut-offs and T-shirts. She could wear a bed sheet and still make you catch your breath.

I wondered how she made it through each day. Wherever she went, whatever she did, male eyes peeled off her clothes. I suddenly knew why she popped up here at eight in the morning. Later in the day, when all my friends arrived, her presence would turn my backyard into Boner Beach.

She reached for the library book I had dropped on the grass. For an instant, her bronze hair passed only inches from my face. A scent wafted off her. Not perfume. Hot sun on skin and palm oil and maybe vanilla. I could have breathed her in all day.

She opened my book. "*The Sea Wolf?* What's it about?"

Ah, firm ground at last. Jack London's world was as familiar to me as my own neighborhood. My tongue got brave. "It's about a sea captain named Wolf Larsen and his crew. They're the scum of the earth."

"Why would he have a crew like that?"

21

"He says he'd rather rule in hell than serve in heaven."

Her left eyebrow arched up. In a measured, academic voice, she said, "That would explain why people become teachers." She held the expression.

Wow, she was sarcastic too. I liked her more and more. I imitated her teacher face and we stayed frozen like that for several seconds until we couldn't hold in the giggles any longer. Those honey-colored eyes connected with mine like I was a real person. Girls her age treated me and my friends like lepers. They would throw rocks at us if they could get away with it. But not her. She stared right at me as if I might say something interesting.

This close, I noticed that one of her front teeth had a small chip. The crisp bridge of her nose flattened near the middle. If she hadn't been looking directly at me, I would not have seen the slight crookedness that showed her nose had once been broken. Rather than detracting from her beauty, her tiny imperfections added to it. She looked real, not like some magazine pin-up.

She ran long fingers back through her short hair, making the silver sunstreaks more prominent. "How cold you think the water is?"

"Well, it's what we beach dwellers call refreshing." In truth, this early in the morning, it was heart attack cold.

"Let's get refreshed," she said. "Or do you want to read?"

Just like that. As if we'd known each other for years. As if what I wanted to do even mattered. If I said I wanted to read, would she sit there with me? No, that would be pushing it. She was seventeen and I was just a twerp.

"No, I'll go."

Hadn't she heard about the body? It was possible. Unless you lived along the shore, you wouldn't have seen the police boats. The morning newspaper had nothing about the dead girl. I assumed the police still hadn't identified her. It was like she had disappeared into a time warp.

The neighborhood gossips had been wagging their tongues yesterday, but somehow my involvement hadn't been revealed. Should I tell her?

How many chances to be with an angel would I get in my life? I kept my mouth shut.

My brain locked at the realization I would have to take off my T-shirt in front of her. I pondered how I could get from the grass to the water in the shortest possible time. I had a good tan, but my ribs showed and I had no chest whatsoever. My father called me string bean. Right now I hated my string bean body.

She turned away and stepped onto the sand and into the clear water until it reached her thighs. My God, she had the neatest, tightest pair of buttocks I had ever seen, and believe me, in the last year I'd microscopically examined just about every issue of *Playboy* ever published. I shook myself out of my religious experience and used the opportunity of Sharon turning away to throw off my shirt. I ran down the sloping sand and dove out to deep water. When I surfaced, I could barely breathe from the icy shock, but that was better than having her scrutinize my skinny frame. With water up to her waist, Sharon held her arms across her chest, as if she could delay the inevitable.

"Would you rather we went out in my boat 'til the water warms up?"

She glanced at the cratered hulk tied to the dock. "Some boat. I'd rather swim."

"It's better if you just do it all at once," I said.

Her eyes narrowed and an impish smile twisted her face. "Would that make it even more refreshing?" In the moment before she let go with her legs and dropped her body under the water, I saw her bikini top. It looked like fingertips pushed out against the smooth white of the fabric.

When her head surfaced, both her hands sluiced the water off her face. With no make-up and her short hair swept back, she looked like a tomboy. That made it less nerve-wracking for me, like maybe I was just with a girl and not a goddess.

She started with an overhand stroke, the smoothest Australian Crawl I had ever seen. After two minutes, I lagged twenty feet behind. She looked back. "Whatsa matter, Jake? I heard you were fast."

I poured it on and kept up with her, but I had a feeling she was trying not to embarrass me. The one thing I thought I was really good at and a girl was showing me up. Swimming that fast, maybe she'd get a cramp and I'd have to save her. Mouth-to-mouth resuscitation on Sharon Young. Yeah, dream on.

We swam into a wide part of the lake. A breeze rippled the surface into a million prisms. Sharon turned, the sun firing the droplets on her face into a crystal mask. "Where should we go?"

"Need a rest?"

"No. Well, a little."

"We can rest right out here."

Her eyes danced. "Are you crazy?"

"No, follow me." I lined up several landmarks on shore, paddling around until my toes brushed against sand. Finding the shallow spot, I stood up. The water came to my neck.

Sharon swam up to the sand bar and stood next to me. "Neat," she said.

I felt around until I found the flat boulder at the middle of the ridge. It was big enough for us both to stand on with the water just at chest level. Even though she had three years on me, we stood about the same height.

"This is kind of my secret," I said.

The pixie grin came back. "I won't tell anybody."

"I use this island when we play water tag. I come out here and rest, but I stay low. My friends think I'm treading water. When someone comes out to get me, I take off like a shot."

"So maybe we shouldn't stand up so high in case someone sees us." She settled lower in the water.

"Yeah," I said, following suit, but wishing that bikini top had stayed at the surface. When we kicked off to continue our swim, her leg brushed against my thigh. Her skin felt warmer than seemed possible in the cool water.

CHAPTER 5

As the sun clocked higher in the cloudless sky, I forgot how big a celebrity I accompanied. We paddled to the headwaters of the lake into an untouched world of lily pads and yellow sandbars. I showed her cold springs that spewed white sand up from deep in the earth, forming underwater cones like anthills. We caught a big painted turtle and set him on the beach to see how fast he could run.

Other boys my age would just as soon crush a turtle as watch it, so I kept this world to myself. At first, I watched Sharon with some nervousness, but her fingers held the turtle delicately. Her eyes lit up when I pointed out holes in the sandstone cliffs where swallows nested. We watched them commute back and forth, feeding their young.

The gap in our ages didn't seem so vast now. Some door inside me opened a tiny bit and I glimpsed a friend different from any I had ever imagined. A girl for a friend?

We lazed in the warm water off a sandbar with grains so small it felt like we were laying on butter. Deep green lily pads undulated on the water's surface. Sunlight transformed the overhanging leaves of birches and maples into glowing emeralds. Willow branches the color of weathered copper whipped gently in the breeze. Even the air smelled green as if we had found the chlorophyll factory that supplied the world.

As the cliff swallows flitted around us, I stared at the sandstone wall, remembering sunset on the evening before I hooked into the body. Rowing away from this part of the lake, I had heard a loud racket from the blue herons shrieking. What had disturbed them? I halfway remembered a scream. And the next day there's a dead girl in the lake? My eyes wandered across the red cliffs. I wished I had paid more attention.

Sharon's voice brought me back. "You're not like other boys."

Flipping my gaze back to her, I shaded my eyes with my hands. "What do you mean?"

"You're not trying to touch me."

"Guys try to touch you?"

She pursed her lips and cocked her head. "What do you think?"

I stared down at the wet yellow granules between us. "Well, uh, wearing stuff like that doesn't help." I vaguely flipped a hand at her bikini.

"Jake, do you wear clothes when you take a bath?"

I laughed. "No."

"So, why do they call these things bathing suits?"

"I don't know."

"When you're swimming, wouldn't it feel better, wouldn't you go faster with nothing on?"

"Well, uh, yeah."

"In this bikini it feels like I'm wearing nothing when I'm in the water. I love that feeling. Like I'm flying. Like I'm free."

I prayed my tan hid the blush that screamed from my skin. "Oh," was all I could think to say.

The imp smile took over her face. "You've never skinny-dipped?"

For the second time that day my tongue died. A razor clam in the shallows suddenly drew my interest.

"You haven't, have you?" Her pale eyebrows arched to ridiculous heights.

I tilted up my face enough to peek from under my brows and answered by shaking my head.

"You want to now? There isn't a soul around."

Oh, God, maybe I could slip quietly off the sand bar and just drown.

"It's no big deal. C'mon." She reached her arms behind her back.

Skinny-dip? Oh, great. I had a grand total of three pubes. All I could think of was the way the older guys made fun of me when we took showers in gym class. This would be a hundred times worse.

I heard a faint snap and the tension of the cloth across her breasts diminished.

Oh, this was going from the best day of my life to the worst. After this humiliation I'd have to leave the state.

Before she could release her top, I blurted, "N-no. That's okay."

"Scared?"

I must have had sunstroke or heat exhaustion or something worse. That would have to be my excuse later. Every guy I knew would sell himself into slavery to trade places with me. I said, "Sharon, why are you doing this? You said I was different. Now you're trying to make me just like all those other guys." I threw some heat into my voice at the end and prayed that my ploy would work.

We stared at each other a long time before she re-fastened her top. The corners of her mouth turned down. "Sometimes I don't know why I do things." She gazed across the water for a minute, then turned to me and stroked her long fingers across my cheek. Just once. "You really are sweet. I'm sorry."

I felt like I had just avoided being hit by a bus. "Try to keep your clothes on." I said it as a joke, but I regretted it because she looked like I'd smacked her with a stick.

She nodded and said, "You're right." She rolled onto her stomach, facing me, her chin supported on her hands. The rest of her body sloped down into the water. "We'll be special friends, okay? Just you and me. We'll be just two people who can talk to each other without all that boyfriend-girlfriend foolishness getting in the way. Okay?"

I didn't know what I was getting into, but I didn't care. She owned me. "Sure, but why me?"

Her smile made me giddy. "You brought me into your special little world back here. You're the only boy who treats me like a friend."

"You must have lots of friends."

All that beauty collapsed into a frown. "I wish."

"Guys are always talking to you."

"You think they want to be friends?"

I lifted my hands, palms up. "Sure looks that way. They say stuff. You laugh."

The frown turned to a scowl. "Boyfriends are *not* friends."

"Why not?"

"They only want me for one thing." It was the saddest voice I ever heard.

"Oh," I said. "Don't you have girlfriends?"

"Girls hate me. Their boyfriends drool over me, so they hate me."

I suddenly had a window into a world so different from mine. Nobody drooled over me and I was pretty sure nobody hated me. Well, except for that crazy cop, Rubino. Some people found me annoying, but they were mostly relatives, so it didn't matter.

"You really don't have a close friend?" I said.

"I wish I had someone to talk to, Jake. Someone I could trust."

I gave her my best puppy-dog face.

Her eyes fixed on the sandstone cliffs and in a faint voice she said, "The secrets are getting too hard to keep." She suddenly sounded so much younger than me.

I had never hung out with girls. Talking like this, I felt like I was in deep water far from any shore. Did girls talk like this all the time? Or was I witnessing a rare event? I thought beautiful girls had perfect lives. Shouldn't the most beautiful among them have *the* most perfect life? Yet, I was feeling sorry for her.

I wanted to tell her what happened two nights ago. I said, "I have a secret too."

She shifted her gaze toward me and tilted her head.

At the last instant I changed my mind. I had promised the cops not to talk about the body. I said, "I've never spent this much time with a girl."

"How's it going so far?"

I smiled. "Girls are way more complicated than the guys I know."

She rose onto her hands and knees and surged toward me. I didn't know what to make of it. Her eyes loomed close and suddenly her lips planted a kiss on my right cheek. She settled back on her haunches. "You really are the most amazing sweetie pie," she said.

For a moment, I was engulfed in that special sun-smell that seemed unique to her. My nostrils flared and I inhaled her. No question about it. I would be her slave for life.

The day flew by in a blur until she said, "What time do you think it is?"

I squinted up through the tree canopy. "About three-thirty."

A shadow crept across her clean features. "Do we have to swim the whole way back? I need to get home before my father."

I had the same problem. My mother got home from work around four o'clock. Her strict rule was that my little brother, Paul, and I could swim off our beach, but only if we were together or we had a swimming buddy. We were not allowed to leave the property. Ignoring these rules usually presented no problem. If we got home before my mother, we could revise history any way we wanted, but if either of us wasn't there we learned what steaks felt like on the charcoal grill.

"Follow me." That's what my mouth said, but I was ready to spend the rest of my life right there. These hours had been like nothing else I had ever experienced.

I knew all the trails in the woods. We marched single file through dappled shade, over crackling leaves and downy moss. Sharon didn't speak. I worried I had done something wrong. As we came to the end of the trail, her lips pressed together. I said, "We just have to swim across the cove to get your clothes."

The shouts and laughs of my friends echoed across the cove.

Five of them fired mud bombs at each other in the shallows, my younger brother among them. Super-fat Dennis Gumm rumbled down the dock. A barrage of mud bombs spattered into him before he cannon-balled off the end of the dock to splash an enormous crater in the lake.

The next five minutes flashed through my mind. My nerdliness would be erased when word spread of me emerging from the lake with a water goddess. Thoughts of permanent coolness eclipsed everything.

Until I glanced at Sharon. Her face stiffened into a mask. She held her arms across her chest. I imagined her dashing up my beach and across the gauntlet of my lawn with five pairs of hungry eyes shredding off what little fabric covered her.

"I have to get home," she almost whispered.

I weighed permanent enshrinement in the halls of coolness against what my new friend would pay for it.

"This way," I said.

We skirted the inhabited areas of our hamlet. When I led her onto a graveled street, she said, "I know where I am now."

She just kept going. No good-bye, no promise to meet again. Her bare feet made little crunching sounds in the gravel as she picked her way around sunny patches where the asphalt oozed sticky and hot.

I don't know what I expected as I watched her sway into the distance. When she was a hundred yards away, she glanced over her shoulder and disappeared around a corner. I wondered how I would explain her T-shirt and cut-offs as I trudged back through the woods to my house.

CHAPTER 6
July 4, 1965

Big-letter headlines screamed across the morning newspaper. Instead of the usual sappy Independence Day garbage they ran, they had front page pictures of the dead girl. The police had released her name. And mine. Early in the morning the phone had begun jangling. Reporters wanted to talk to me. My mother was home because of the holiday, so she screened the calls. Finally, annoyed, she took the phone off the hook.

Paul glued his face to the TV as stations in New York and Philadelphia flashed photos of the dead girl and spun their tales of mystery and horror. I couldn't watch.

I couldn't eat. Not from the publicity, but because the dead girl was Janey Young, Sharon's older sister. When I pulled her face out of the water, I didn't have the slightest glimmer of recognition. Not that I knew her personally, but I knew of her. She was a meteor that streaked across the heavens to awe us primitives. I would stare for those few seconds as her perfect face peered out of a passing car. Or I'd stop in my tracks to watch her glide past in a department store. As amazing as Sharon was, her older sister was even more breathtaking.

Knowing she was dead shattered my view of the world. That such beauty could wind up a pale horrible corpse hooked on my fishing lure made me doubt the existence of God. And I had spent all of yesterday with her sister. I felt so creepy I wanted to throw up.

Today was usually the biggest day of my year, the day I blew my brains out in a non-stop gunpowder-induced madness. Instead, I moped around the house.

After dinner, I didn't dare go outside. A mint-green '63 Impala sat in front of my house. Two heads bobbed inside, yapping about whatever people yapped about to kill time. Occasionally, they turned their hopeful pie faces toward the house. More damn reporters. I needed to get away, but not by the street.

I left the house through the walk-out basement door at the back and hustled down to the dock. I carried Sharon's T-shirt and shorts in a paper bag. The news

31

hawks hadn't thought of watching the water. I rowed toward the swamp and hid *Crater Face* under a willow that grew along the shore. A short hike brought me to the end of a street near the Young house.

I scouted for reporters, but either they had already gotten what they wanted or had been scared off by Sharon's father, because I didn't see anybody camped out front.

I didn't know what I would say, but I wanted to tell Sharon how sorry I was about her sister. What a way to start a friendship. Head down, I knocked on the front door. Janey Young's death had no connection to me; I just found her body. Yet I felt like I had done something wrong and needed to atone.

Knocking again, I thought I heard movement inside, but nobody came to the door. The skin at the back of my neck prickled as I marched down the steps. As I turned the corner on my way to Eddie's I saw old man Young at the back of the yard, poking at a smoky fire with a metal pole. I had seen him burning trash other times. The tang of burning leaves was something I liked, but Buddy Young's garbage always made a killer stench. When we were younger, Eddie tried to convince me that Buddy Young and his son, Ralph, burned dogs and cats and sometimes babies in the back yard.

My movement must have caught his eye. He stared straight at me. Having that hulk's eyes on me gave me the heebie-jeebies. Slipping around the hedges on the corner, I hustled next door to Eddie's. He wasn't home and his mother didn't know where he was.

This plan had gone to crap. Sweat rolled down my forehead and into my eyebrows as I trudged to the end of the street and shuffled through the woods, no real goal in mind beyond getting back to my boat and on the water where it was cooler. Halfway to the shore I heard crackling in the underbrush behind me. I turned and listened, hearing only the peeping of thrushes and a slight rustling of a breeze high in the tree branches. Whoever it was had stopped. My eyes scanned back and forth, but I detected nobody.

Until now I hadn't truly confronted the probability that Janey Young had been murdered by someone who maybe lived nearby, who passed me on the street, who bought groceries in the local Acme Supermarket. I had no idea who this someone was.

Being alone in the woods sent a chill through me despite the humid July heat that hung even in the shade. I felt eyes crawling over my skin. I almost shouted, "Show yourself," but I knew this shadow man wouldn't and maybe if he saw I was scared, he would come for me. Maybe my body wouldn't be found. Maybe he would tie cinder blocks to me and sink me in the deepest part of the lake.

Maybe I should get out of there.

I turned and ran.

I have never been afraid on the lake or in the woods or in the deepest enclaves of the swamp, but now I had to go, get away, run. My insides squirmed with primitive fear.

My heartbeat drummed in my ears as I scrambled through dense foliage that stung and ripped at my bare arms and legs. Branches clung to me, tried to pull me down like in a nightmare. I had stumbled off the trail and ran wildly. A branch tore the paper bag from my grip. I couldn't go back for Sharon's clothes, couldn't stop running.

All I could think of was to get to *Crater Face*, push it away from the shadows, and row into bright sunlight. My teeth hurt, I ran so hard. That wasn't good. I had a heart murmur, some kind of valve problem. It never bothered me except when I really pushed myself. Like now. I hoped I wouldn't faint. I had a problem with fainting.

Breaking through a stand of elderberry bushes, I rejoiced at seeing the weeping willow along the shore, the shiny bow of *Crater Face* peaking out from under its hanging branches. I leaned into the willow's leafy streamers, parting them with my hands. I couldn't see more than a foot in front of my face. Bending down, I grabbed the bow of my boat, preparing to shove it off the beach. My peripheral vision erupted in little bursts of light and I heard the sound of wind in my ears. *No, not now. Please not now!*

I crouched and leaned on the edge of the bow. If I fainted, I would be easy prey for the one who followed me.

I took deep breaths and let my head hang down. In a few seconds the flashing lights relented.

I had difficulty shoving *Crater Face* off the shore. It seemed heavier. I stepped onto the front seat as the lush strings of the willow branches slapped against my face. When I cleared the branches, I was shocked to see Sharon Young in the stern. How had I not sensed her? It was as if she radiated no energy, as if she was a hole in space. She was there, but everything about her said she wasn't.

She looked up. "Row, Jake."

Something in her voice scared me even more. I dropped onto the metal seat and grabbed the oars. In seconds, we skimmed across the surface, headed out from the hulking hills, away from the shadows.

The sun hit us and I let the boat drift as I scanned the shoreline over Sharon's shoulder. I saw nobody, but I could still feel eyes on me. My breathing slowed. My teeth stopped hurting.

I began rowing again, but slowly this time, making for the center of the lake. My brain began to work. I said, "How did you find my boat?"

"Saw you at my house. When you left, I crawled down the rose trellis from the back porch. Thought you might be going back to the lake and I remembered that hidden spot you showed me."

Her cheek was swollen. I blurted, "Who hit you?"

A flash of fear widened her eyes. Her mouth said, "Nobody. I...I fell."

"Tell me."

Her gaze shifted to the far shore and she did not answer. I turned downstream toward the widest part of the lake and concentrated on rowing, on putting distance between us and the eyes in the trees. Why did I think it was a he? And why did I think he was the murderer of Janey Young? Was anyone even there? Was I just a stupid kid, scared of my shadow?

"Show me, Jake."

Cryptic as it sounded, I knew what she meant. "Are you sure?"

"Show me."

I scanned nearby hilltops and docks and the largest trees. Adjusting my course, I rowed for a few minutes, then dragged my oars deep, pushed hard, and brought the boat to a stop. "Here."

"You're sure?"

I nodded, not trusting my voice. For three days I had somehow made myself not think too deeply about finding Janey Young's body. I made my life go on as if I could blot out such a thing, distracting myself with thoughts of the Fourth of July, but now, taking Sharon to the place I found her sister's body, I remembered the heaviness on my fishing line, that porcelain skin, the polka dots. I tried to make my memory stop before it got to those eyes, but I couldn't stop it. It showed me those gaping eye holes, the black hair, the tattered lips.

A chill ran through me. Why was I scared more now, three days after finding the body? The answer was simple. It had become real. Maybe I had just had a brush with the killer in the woods. But why would the killer be interested in me? All I did was find the body.

I turned my head and gazed at the opposite shore and prayed that Sharon wouldn't ask me to describe what happened.

She didn't. We sat for several minutes, silent. She scanned the water, the clouds, the beach line. Was she trying to etch it all into her memory, freeze it in time? She pulled a silver locket out of the front pocket of her jeans, leaned over the side, and dropped it into the green water. For a moment it flashed, then like a perch ambushed by a pike, the locket was swallowed in the green depths.

My new friend suffered. I had to find a way to help her.

Was I putting myself in danger?

The magic of summer vacation paled. It felt like the day I learned that Santa Claus was really my parents with wrapping paper and a lot of BS.

Later that night, I sat on my back porch and listened to explosions from all over the neighborhood. I didn't lift a finger to join in the mayhem. It was the worst Independence Day I ever had. And some deep part of me knew it would be the last time I even cared.

"Jake, stay out of those woods."

"I don't need you spookin' me again."

"Well, somethin' needs to scare your freakin' stupid ass."

"You're a basket case, Eddie."

"Yeah? Well, my name was in the papers too. My old man wanted to kill me when reporters showed up at the door. I'm stayin' right here, in my house, and tryin' to forget the whole freakin' thing."

"Eddie, can we open a window? That glue is killing me." Eddie was assembling another model plane. He had dozens of them hanging from the joists above us. I usually stayed out of his basement when he used airplane glue. The sharp stink of it made me feel like somebody was pulling out the hairs from inside my nose.

"Dammit, you know the freakin' windows are painted shut. You'd need a jackhammer to get 'em open."

"It's giving me a headache."

Eddie wrapped a rubber band around a tiny piece he had attached to the fuselage of the jet fighter. "C'mon." We stomped up the timber stairs and out of the basement dankness into the blast furnace of July. Eddie led me around the side of his house into the shade at the back where we plopped into two wicker chairs. Eddie's transistor radio sat on an overturned milk crate between the chairs. He flicked it on. The Beach Boys were asking Rhonda for help.

Eddie's golden retriever pranced up and presented his ears for me to scratch. "You just give Duke a bath? His hair is soft as mink."

"When have you ever touched a mink?"

"Well, never."

"Then how do you know what it feels like? It might feel like steel wool for all you know." Eddie scowled across his yard at the hedgerow.

"What the hell's wrong with you, Eddie? What are you so jumpy about?"

He shot me a look like I just farted. "Right, I got no reason to be jumpy." Then he pointed. "Duke won't go near that corner of the yard. Know why?"

I shook my head.

"Old man Young." Eddie's back yard shared the hedgerow with the Young yard. "His fire pit's just on the other side of the hedge. Duke was nosin' around in it. Young got pissed at him, said he was barkin'. You know Duke doesn't bark, but that bastard sprayed him with ammonia. Duke went nuts. The smell. Now he won't go near that freakin' yard."

"When did this happen?"

"Couple days ago. You go over there, you can still smell it."

I squinted. "Where you goin' with this?"

He whispered. "Jake, I hear lots of crap comin' from that house."

"What?"

"It's a zoo over there. Stay away from those people." Eddie leaned toward me and lowered his voice. "Old man Young's a mean-ass sonofabitch. You ask me, he killed Janey."

I didn't hang around. Eddie was such a nervous wreck, I couldn't stand him.

Trudging toward home, trying to ignore the heat, I had gone maybe a block when the earth under my feet started to vibrate. In a few seconds the humid air carried the deep burbling sound of a powerful engine. I turned back and saw Charles J. Dougal, Jr. roaring toward me in his souped-up '56 Ford Fairlane. I loved his car, though I had never been inside it; I had dubbed it *The Cherry Bomb* because of its color. He whipped the Ford to my side of the street and skidded to a stop so his window was exactly even with me, parked on the wrong side of the street; Chaz considered traffic laws mere suggestions.

"Hey, Chaz."

Blond surfer hair, blue eyes, and one of those Cary Grant chins made Chaz the biggest heart throb in high school. He wore his official hot rod guy uniform: black leather boots, Levi's, and a T-shirt so tight you could see every muscle in his torso.

"Jake, wanna see my new Holleys?"

"Sure." I had no idea what Holleys were, but Chaz seemed so happy, I didn't want to sour his mood. Pissing off Chaz was never a good idea. He leapt out of his car and popped the hood. Mostly I saw chrome. Anything that wasn't chrome was blue. I recognized the radiator, but the rest was a Rube Goldberg puzzle to me. "Your engine is cleaner than my room."

"Whaddya think of those Holleys?"

I had no idea what part of the engine to look at, so I said, "What are they for?"

"Best carbs in the world. Suck in more air, get more power, make this bitch go like hell."

Yeah, I still didn't know which thingees to look at. So, I stepped back and admired the whole package. "This is really a great rod, Chaz." It really was. The red paint was so deep and perfect, I could see myself in it.

Out of the top of his right boot, Chaz pulled the black-handled switchblade he always carried. He flicked it open and used the blade to turn a screw on something. "Idle's a little low. That should fix it." He put the knife back in his boot and said, "C'mon, get in."

A request from Chaz was like an order from the Commander in Chief. I didn't dare say no, not that I was tempted to. None of my friends had ever been in *The Cherry Bomb*. This was quite an honor. In five seconds that Fairlane flew so fast, I was afraid to look up. Chaz thought I was admiring the dashboard. "Go on. Crank up the radio. It's primo."

I flicked the dial and that limey bastard, Mick Jagger, started screaming about how he couldn't get no satisfaction. I hoped he continued to suffer unsatisfied because I hated that rubber-lipped jack-off. From the way the sound juggled my guts, Chaz must have installed bass speakers the size of washtubs in his trunk.

"Leave that on. Cool, huh?" When Chaz grinned like that, you'd have to be a corpse not to feel good along with him.

"Yeah." I turned the volume down a few notches. Chaz threw me some steel-eye and I turned the volume back up. Our neighborhood, Lakeview, disappeared in a blur. In no time we hit Route 130, a four-lane highway, and Chaz really opened it up. I had never been in an airplane, but I imagined this was how it felt. A hurricane whipped through the open windows. Chaz had never looked happier.

I pointed to the top of the windshield. "How come you don't have a rearview mirror?"

Chaz laughed. "When you can go this fast, it don't matter what's behind you."

Chaz punched in the dashboard cigarette lighter, reached into the rolled up sleeve on his left arm, and pulled out his Marlboros. As he lit up, I smiled. We were an odd pair. Chaz was eighteen; I was fourteen. Normally, I should have been cannon fodder to get beat on by guys like him. Through a fluke we met in sophomore English class. Chaz had been held back two years and I had skipped two grades in grammar school. Our lives met in the middle.

Being the class clown, Chaz appreciated a good audience. And I was his best audience. I landed in the principal's office more than he did because Chaz would crack me up and I wouldn't be able to stop laughing. Somehow that made us friends. Well, maybe not like hang-around-together-friends. I was more his mascot. The real wise-asses knew he liked me, which probably saved me from a dozen ass-whippings in the past year.

"Hey, Chaz."

"Yah?"

"Can I ask you something?"

"No, I will not take you to a whore house. You're a freakin' minor."

"Not that. About Janey Young."

He flicked an icy glance at me. What had I done wrong?

Chaz floored it and now the roar of the engine made it impossible to hear him even if he had tried to answer me. We flew for a couple minutes, then Chaz hit the brakes, rounded a turn and said, "I need a burger." He turned the car so fast, I slid across the front seat and slammed into my door. What the hell? Were we crashing?

When I looked up, the car sat motionless in front of a Stewart's Root Beer stand. In Chaz-world even the laws of physics were mere suggestions. The dust cloud from the gravel driveway caught up to us and drifted across the parking lot like fog.

A black-haired waitress in tight white shorts and a tight red blouse skated up to the driver side window and hooked a tray to it. She didn't look much older than me. I wondered how many miles a day she put on those roller skates.

"Some entrance, Chaz. What'll you have?" she said. Her gray eyes gazed at Chaz as if he were the only man left on earth.

Chaz turned toward her and gave her a Hollywood grin. "Whaddaya got?"

She chewed her gum faster and leaned closer to the window. "What I got is a short shift tonight, Chaz. I'm off at nine."

Chaz turned away from the window as if she hadn't spoken. "Whaddaya want, Jake?"

"I don't have any money."

"Did I ask ya for money?" He turned back to the window. "Babe, how 'bout a coupla cheeseburgers, Cokes, fries?"

What she gave Chaz wasn't a smile. I don't know what it was, half leer, half I hate your guts. She glided through the cars toward the building. My view of her legs got blocked by a blue Buick convertible that pulled up on my side.

"One of your admirers?" I said.

"Yeah, maybe I'll come back later and give her a tour of my back seat." Chaz turned toward me and leaned back against his door. "So, what about Janey?"

"Do you think someone killed her?"

He stared out the windshield.

"I mean, Chaz, why would someone want to kill her? She was just a teenage girl. What could she possibly do to anybody?"

Chaz lit another cigarette from the remains of the first one and took a long pull on it. With smoke drifting out of his mouth, he said, "Some women make men crazy." He stared out the windshield for a long time, occasionally taking a drag on his Marlboro and letting the smoke spill slowly out his nostrils.

I was afraid to break the silence. I had never seen Chaz so still.

Finally, the waitress rolled up and put our food on the window tray. "That's two eighty."

Chaz handed her a five. "I'll give you the rest of your tip later, Doll." His dimples blazed at full power.

I thought she would jump in through the window. When she skated away, her thin hips rolled back and forth more than before. She beamed a smile over her shoulder at Chaz. I could have gone up in flames and she wouldn't have noticed me.

As I unwrapped my cheeseburger, I said, "You think it was an accident? Maybe Janey couldn't swim?"

"She could swim like a fish."

I didn't want to ask how he knew that.

"Maybe she was diving and hit her head."

"Swimming with a dress on? Get serious." Chaz stared at me with the most intense look I'd ever seen on his face. "You think everybody's a good guy like you, but they're not."

"What do you mean?"

"People do strange shit, Jake."

CHAPTER 8
July 7, 1965

Two years ago, the first time Uncle Frank delivered my fireworks, my mother went nuts. It took all my persuasive powers and the backing of my father to calm her down. Dad had the perfect line. "Laura, I laid down the law to him. If he messes up, I throw all his fireworks in the lake." To me, he said, "I don't care what you do, just do it out on the lake. You cause a house-fire in the neighborhood and you'll be looking for another home."

My father rarely made threats, so I never ignored them. He had fought the Japanese in World War II and he had a punch like a bulldozer. When he worked out on the heavy bag that hung from a beam in our basement, I thought the chain would break. Other than a slap on the ass when I was little, he had never let fly with anything harder and I wanted it to stay that way.

So, when all hell broke loose, it broke loose on the lake. At night.

Without my depraved leadership, my friends had a dud for July 4th. They nagged me every day for something spectacular to round out the holiday. Even though I had been depressed as hell on the holiday, the passage of three days whetted my appetite for mayhem. I finally gave in and declared a *Ben-Hur* night.

We got the idea from the movie we'd seen years before. In it Romans use catapults to hurl flaming balls at enemy ships during a naval battle. Fire. Romans. Roman candles. The logic of what we had to do was simple.

My friend Kendall lived across the cove. Nobody knew his first name. He was the first one-name person I ever heard of. Kendall was a head taller than everybody and so skinny he made me look like a body builder. His hair. Oh, my God, his hair. It looked like a brown poodle had died on his head. He resembled Art Garfunkle, but he couldn't sing, thank God. His voice sounded like a frog talking through a sewer pipe.

Kendall owned a white lifeguard boat from the Jersey shore, a wooden monster that must have weighed half a ton. It could hold ten of us easily. My nimble twelve-foot aluminum boat against Kendall's behemoth was a strategic match made in heaven.

Three nights after Independence Day, at ten o'clock, we met in the middle of the lake. In the moonlight the two boats looked like ghosts hovering on the inky water. My crew was Eddie and Steve, both slingshot experts. Earlier in the day, Steve and I practically had to beg Eddie to come out on the water. He was way more spooked than I was about finding the body, but free cherry bombs changed his mind. No way I was going into a water battle without Eddie. Kendall had some older kids with him, faceless up-and-comers who thought their greater age made up for skill.

Their waterproof fuses made cherry bombs my weapon of choice for *Ben-Hur* nights. Once they're lit, nothing is going to stop them from exploding. Eddie, Steve, and I came prepared with dried cattail tops – we called them punks – that burned for a half hour with a hot ember capable of instantly lighting the lacquer-coated fuse of a cherry bomb. We saw a flash of matches from Kendall's boat. No preliminaries.

Eddie cackled. "Shee-it. They only have matches." Advantage us. If we forced Kendall's crew to keep his boat moving, the breeze of their passage would make it tough to light matches.

A few perfunctory cherry bombs landed in the space between us. Eddie said, "Those freakin' amateurs, they're just throwin' 'em."

I manned the oars while Eddie loaded a cherry bomb into his Wham-O slingshot, pulled back the pouch, and stood motionless as Steve touched his punk to the fuse. As soon as the fuse hissed, Eddie released. This was the teamwork of long practice. Sparks arced through the darkness toward the shadowy hull of our enemy.

Eddie was good. The cherry bomb landed a foot from Kendall's boat and blossomed like a yellow flower just under the surface of the water, blasting spray ten feet into the air. Kendall's crew howled when the water hit them. Before the spray cleared, Eddie dropped another cherry bomb in the same place, and another, soaking Kendall's crew as the blasts echoed back and forth from the surrounding hills.

"Let them try to light their freakin' matches now," Eddie shrieked.

I pulled *Crater Face* close enough that we didn't need slingshots. By hand, we tossed cherry bombs all around Kendall's boat, drenching everyone on board, making it impossible for them to retaliate. Eddie miscalculated and a cherry bomb landed in the stern of the surf boat and bounced around the hull, spitting sparks like a pinwheel as the fuse burned down.

Kendall's crew started swearing and screaming and two of them jumped overboard. Oh, this was sweet. The cherry bomb went off and we had a flash image of Kendall and some other guy cringing in the bow. Then it got ugly.

A tiny flame appeared on Kendall's boat followed by a spray of sparks. "Look out, Jake, he's got a lighter," Steve hissed.

"Bastard set us up," Eddie shouted. Kendall had intentionally made us overconfident and sucked us in close with his matches ploy. Now we would pay.

Fountains of gold sparks shot out from Kendall's boat and lit us up. This was bad. I screamed, "Steve, grab the other oar. Quick!"

I fumbled with one oar as Steve dropped onto the seat next to me. Before we could dig the oars into the water, a sizzling red ball shot a foot over our heads. "Duck!" Eddie screamed.

We hauled on the oars and the light aluminum boat leaped three feet. More flaming balls flew past us. They had at least four candles going and each Roman candle held twenty balls. I should know. I had made the sale. We were in for it.

Some flaming balls hissed as they hit the water while other slapped into the side of my boat. A green ball hit the opposite hull and bounced into the bottom, sputtering and spinning and sending sparks all over.

"Eddie, grab the box. Grab it! It's open!"

He knew what I meant. If sparks got into our box of fireworks, we'd go up like the finale.

Eddie stomped the spitting Roman candle ball. The sickly stink of burning flip-flop now joined the sharp tang of burnt gunpowder. Eddie flipped the lid down on the metal toolbox that held our fireworks. They were now safe.

An incandescent blue ball smacked into the top of my head, hissing as it passed. I dipped my hand in the water and slapped my scalp. The stench of singed hair now joined the rest of the nostril-assaulting smells. With my crewcut, there wasn't much to burn, but I'd have another welt.

Crater Face pulled out of range of Kendall's attack. My aluminum rowboat was a great sprinter, but once Kendall's heavier boat got up to speed, he could outrun me in a straight race. The trick with evading Kendall was to change direction, to use my boat's nimbleness.

The two guys who had jumped overboard hauled themselves back into Kendall's boat and grabbed the oars. The behemoth plowed toward us, but we had a good lead.

We turned to come across Kendall's bow and sat dead in the water. Time to get serious. My crew donned our snorkeling masks. We looked stupid, but the facemasks made our eyes invulnerable to even a direct hit from a Roman candle ball. As they closed in, Kendall's crew also donned swimming goggles and snorkeling masks. Kendall put on a full-face welder's mask. He looked like Doctor Doom. We all looked like a bunch of idiots.

Steve, Eddie, and I lit our Roman candles and started blasting as the other boat approached. Kendall tried to turn, but his hulk was too unwieldy and he realized that if he turned, he'd give us a bigger target to shoot at. The best his crew could do was dig oars into the water and slow down. They stopped about twenty feet from us.

Somebody over there got a candle lit and we had a point blank shootout. We ducked as red and green and blue balls flashed across the gap. Steve squealed as a ball crashed into his belly. He leaned over the side and splashed water on his T-shirt.

Kendall's crew was already soaked, so when they got hit nobody erupted in flames.

"Bastards. They pay now." I grabbed a fat rocket from the tool box and, holding it by the launching stick, lit the fuse off my Roman candle. The damn thing whistled and ripped across the gap. Kendall's crew ducked in unison to avoid a haircut. The rocket hit the water on the far side of Kendall's boat and twirled under the surface. When it exploded it shot a geyser twenty feet high. The shock wave stung my bare feet through the aluminum deck.

Now it was an endless cascade of sparks and burning balls and explosions. We screamed in fear at the return fire. We screamed with rage and joy and the mindless animal instincts of war.

Eddie shouted, "Let's finish these jackoffs," as the two boats drifted closer together.

We dumped cherry bombs into Kendall's boat; his crew threw strings of Black Cats into my boat. The explosions made one continuous noise, like the ripping of a giant piece of canvas. Everybody jumped overboard. The Roman candles hissed when they hit the water. They kept burning and shooting out balls as they descended into the depths, surrounding us with a pulsating glow from below.

The explosions that raged in the boats tore the night to shreds.

Finally the racket stopped, except for the ringing in my ears. All of us laughed hysterically. We hung onto the boats and rested in the warm water. Sulphurous bubbles burst around us from the still-firing Roman candles far below. It smelled like the boys' room after the school cafeteria served sloppy-Joes.

"Did you see that?" Steve crowed. "It looked like an atom bomb went off."

Eddie's dry voice responded in the dark. "Almost as big as one of your farts."

"Kiss my ass."

"It's too big, Mister Plumpmeister. If I got close to it, gravity would suck me in and I'd never get away."

Suddenly, Steve flailed at the water. "Help, help!"

"What the hell...?" Kendall said.

Steve almost tipped *Crater Face* hauling his bulk up over the side. He flopped into the bottom, gasping.

"What's wrong?" Kendall asked as he hung from the side of his boat.

Eddie and I pulled ourselves out of the water in a panic reflex. Steve panted loudly as I crouched next to him.

"Have you lost your mind?" I said.

"I touched something. In the water."

"Like what?"

"Something big."

Eddie chided, "I told you to stop takin' dumps in the lake."

"No something really big."

"Oh, hell, Thunder-buns, you brushed against my dick," Eddie added.

Steve sat up. "There's something down there."

"Steve, don't go psycho on us. It was probably a turtle," I said, not wanting to give Eddie a reason to think about bodies. The unintended result of my comment was that Kendall and his crew splashed back into his boat like the lake was boiling. We all feared snapping turtles. Some huge ones lived on the bottom. If one of those big bastards chomped into you, it wouldn't let go. They could drown you or take a chunk out of your leg. Maybe sever an artery and you'd bleed to death before you could get to shore. We sat for a minute. Nobody spoke. One lone Roman candle glared from the depths, pumping out pulses of red and blue and green.

"Maybe it's another body," Kendall said with way too much hopefulness.

Oh, great. Just what I wanted to avoid.

Eddie said, "Dammit, Kendall, you watch too many horror movies," but he swiveled his head toward me and I saw the fear on his face in the glow from the water.

More for Eddie's sake than Steve's I said, "Steve, it was a turtle. Stop acting like a girl."

A searchlight lanced the darkness. "Hey, you kids!" boomed from a loudspeaker. It was like a switch had been flipped. Night. Day. We froze in shock.

Seven pairs of eyes swept the south shore. A red and blue bubblegum machine flashed through the trees. All thoughts of turtles and war were obliterated by thoughts of what our parents would do to us.

"We see you. Get over here. Now!"

Nobody moved. We tried to change mental gears. The idea of getting caught was alien to us. Steve whispered, "Jake, my father will beat the livin' crap out of me."

48

"That's easy for him to do, you're so damn full of it," whispered Eddie.

Our boats drifted together and touched with a dull thunk. I had an idea.

"Hey, Kendall," I hissed.

"What?"

"Why should we row over to the cops?"

"Huh?"

"They don't know who we are. Do they have a boat?"

As the realization grew, our mood shifted from fear to arrogance. "No boats," I heard from one of Kendall's crew.

"Kendall, they can't get us. Let's just row over to the other side of the lake."

In a high falsetto voice, Eddie Sparrow shouted, "See you later, officers."

"You kids get over here, right now!"

Both crews pulled on the oars hard and fast and we soon approached the opposite shore, out of range of the spotlight. Sparks flared and war resumed. Now that everyone was soaked, direct hits from Roman candles just caused minor burns. The tempo was even more insane than before. We had a lot of adrenaline to work off.

A searchlight darted through the trees on this side of the lake. "You little bastards get over here, right now! I mean it. Right now!"

As if we were telepathic, like in *Children of the Damned*, all of us turned our fire toward shore. Cherry bombs hissed through the night to send up waterspouts along the beach. Roman candles churned out flaming balls so bright they rendered the cops' searchlight useless. A dense wall of sulphurous smoke poured toward shore. With the smoke as a shield, we rowed away. We watched the angry strobe of the police car speed around the west shore, but before the cops could hail us again, we rowed to a wooded cove and laid low. We had blasted away almost all our ammo anyway.

Eddie hissed, "I can't believe we just did that."

Steve added, "If those cops ever figure out who we are, they'll kill us."

Kendall's voice honked out of the dark, "Want to go catfishin'?" He had a thing about fishing at night for catfish. I don't remember him ever catching any, but he was always game to try.

"You got fishing poles?" Like I should ask. Kendall *always* had a pole or three bouncing around the bottom of his boat.

"Yeah."

"How about bait?"

"Yeah."

Eddie, Steve, and I tied *Crater Face* to Kendall's boat and hopped aboard the bigger vessel. We brought our punks and stuck them in the oarlocks to keep away the mosquitoes. Kendall passed around his can of mosquito repellent and we all took a spritz. Steve immediately said, "You got anything to eat?"

Eddie's voice pierced the dark, "You can eat *me*, Thunderthighs."

"Oh, screw you, Birdbrains."

"My ass is yours to screw, Mr. Homo, right after you eat me."

War was not always waged with gunpowder.

CHAPTER 9
July 8, 1965

Summer mornings followed a pattern. Lay in bed until hunger turned unbearable, then stagger downstairs to the kitchen. If it was a weekend, my mother made pancakes, something I looked forward to all week.

I might have to endure wearing a new shirt bought three sizes too big so that I could "grow into it," but where food was concerned, my parents compensated with little flourishes. We had *real* maple syrup, not that cheapo sugar garbage. I hated that crap.

So much vacation stretched ahead that I didn't even care what day it was. I slipped on a bathing suit and an almost-clean T-shirt and tottered down the stairs. I didn't smell pancakes. Weekday. That meant my mother and father had already gone to work and I was sole proprietor of our holdings.

The kitchen table looked like wolverines had eaten breakfast. Puddles of milk. Soggy corn flakes resembling amoebas crawling across the blue plastic tablecloth. A peach pit. And a napkin with a booger right in the middle of it. A gift from my malicious, soon-to-be-murdered-before-he-sees-his-tenth-birthday little brother.

Fortunately for Paul he was nowhere in sight. As long as he didn't bother me during the day, I didn't care if he was covering the neighborhood with his boogers or building an atomic bomb.

I dumped half a quart of milk into a Cheerios box, tipped it back against my mouth, and powered it down. Instant breakfast and no dishes to clean.

Scanning the first few pages of the newspaper, I found no mention of me. The Janey Young story now focused on the coroner and the police department. I was happy to be forgotten.

I carried a book down the yard to my favorite spot under the maple. After reading the same page six times I put it aside. The water looked inviting, but I didn't feel like swimming. I didn't feel like doing anything. I wanted to see Sharon. I hadn't been with her since she dropped the locket in the lake.

I waited until late afternoon to venture out. Since lunch hour was long over, I figured the chance of her father, Buddy Young, popping home was remote.

The sun baked the asphalt streets to goo. The sharp petroleum tang of it assaulted my sinuses as badly as the day when it had been laid down by teams of sweaty fat guys in guinea-Ts. Those guys had stunk worse than the tar.

Looking up the street was like gazing across the Gobi Desert. The shimmering air rising from the asphalt blurred anything more than two blocks away into a mirage. I hustled from tree to tree, using every pool of shade as haven from the savage sun.

I had prepared some lame explanation of why I wanted to see her, but I got no chance to use it. Sharon answered my knock and said, "Come on in." She wore jean cut-offs with strings hanging down to her knees. Bare feet with no nail polish. She had tied one end of a big red handkerchief around the back of her neck and the other end around her narrow waist so it covered her chest more or less. Mostly less. No way she was wearing a bra under that. Jewels of sweat beaded her skin.

As we passed through the living room, a little white Scottie dog tore in, circled me, sniffed at my sneakers. I scratched his ears and he wagged his tail.

Sharon said, "That's Pee-Wee."

"Your father around?"

"I wouldn't let you in if he was. Want a soda?"

"Sure." I didn't care what flavor. Just being with her was all I needed. She led me into the shadowy kitchen, opened an ancient Kelvinator and came out with two sweating bottles of orange soda. She popped the caps off them with a rusted bottle opener that was the only object on the red linoleum counter. The kitchen had a weird smell, like bad milk and mold.

"Buried my sister yesterday." She just blurted it out. No preliminaries.

"I've never been to a funeral."

"No, I said we buried her. There was no funeral. Just a pine box they lowered into a hole. Me, my father, and my brother, and some old fart who read the Bible. That was it. She got quite a send-off. I'm surprised my father

52

didn't just leave her body at the city dump."

"They didn't get along?"

She shot me steel-eye. "He's cheap, Jake. If it doesn't come in a six pack, he won't buy it."

I stared at the dingy oak floor. What could I say? This house was depressing. It hadn't been painted in a million years. The walls were faded green, more dirt than paint, and the floors looked like they'd been dipped in soot. I could barely see through the windows. It looked like nobody here had cared for a long time.

"Let's go on the porch," she said. I was glad to get out of that kitchen. We sat in director's chairs so threadbare I was afraid I might fall through the seat.

Sharon stared into space for a long time. To hide my nervousness, I gulped down half my soda. The silence finally got to me so I asked the first stupid question that came into my mind. "Where's your mom?"

Sharon turned her face toward me. Her eyes seemed to be looking at something over my shoulder. "She got out a long time ago." She turned away. "She was the only smart one in this family."

We heard a rumble and the crunch of gravel from the driveway. Sharon's eyes narrowed. "Damn, the bastard's home early," she said. Before we could move, a green Ford pick-up truck parked alongside the porch. "Act normal," she said.

Normal? What did that mean? I spent my life trying to be un-normal.

Buddy Young yanked open the screen door with such force I thought the hinges would pop. I wasn't sure he could get through the opening. He looked like one giant muscle with arms thicker than my whole body. By lowering his head and angling his body sideways, he made it through the doorway, but his shoulders still brushed the frame. The screen door slapped shut behind him. The floorboards groaned as he approached.

I had never been this close to Buddy Young and never wanted to be this close again. I tried to look normal. Very normal. So plain-vanilla normal he wouldn't notice me.

His green coveralls showed more grease than cloth. Black streaks ran through his short blond hair as if he had wiped his dirty hands through it. That face looked like a block of concrete, square, thick with a wide nose smashed to one side. Who on this planet had ever had the balls to punch this monster's nose?

"What's this twerp doin' in my house?" As Young passed, he ran the back of his hand up my cheek. "Well, the twerp don't have a beard, so he must not have a dick. I guess you're safe with him."

I pulled back from that hand so fast something clicked in my neck.

"Where's my dinner, girl?" Young eyeballed me.

"I've been out," Sharon said.

"Out? Your mother was never out. When I got home supper was on the table."

"I'm not your wife."

When Young squinted at me, I turned away. He might have read about me in the newspaper. Holy Christmas, I hoped he didn't put two and two together.

He thumped into the kitchen. The refrigerator door opened and thumped closed. A bottle cap jangled across the counter. He reappeared in the doorway, draining half his Pabst Blue Ribbon in one gulp. Pee-Wee scampered around his feet, claws clacking on the oak.

"You feed this dog?"

"Not yet."

"I'm not feedin' it. You don't want to take care of it, I'll kill this damn dog. Wring its scrawny little neck." He lumbered into the living room and turned on the TV.

I had to get out of there. I felt like a real coward when I rose from the chair and said, "I should be getting home." Sharon's mouth twisted down and her eyes locked onto mine. Before she could say anything, I pushed open the screen door. I wasn't proud of myself as I double-timed it across the yard

CHAPTER 10
July 9, 1965

A scream echoed around the cove. It didn't come from any animal I knew. I raced down the hill to the beach and double-timed it three properties over, where I thought the sound had originated. I stopped to listen, but didn't hear anything unusual. Blue Jays pinged like sonar in the trees and flies buzzed by as if everything was normal. That creeped me out more than anything.

Earl Broward's house sprawled on a rise a little back from the shore. The lake breeze shoved the uncut grass back and forth with a sound like rustling paper as I stepped through the dappled shadows under the high oaks at the back of the house. Earl hunkered like a bundle of rags at the top of the path that led down to me.

I climbed the embankment. He didn't look up.

Earl was my age, but a lot smaller. He could have passed for ten. A shiny mane of chestnut hair hung over his face. Some of the older kids teased him with the name Pony Boy. When he finally sensed my presence, his head lifted. The dark circles under his eyes seemed even more pronounced than usual.

"What happened, Earl?"

A long time passed, with him just staring at me. He said, "You really want to know? C'mon." He stood and turned to the screen door at the back of the house. "I'll show you my old man's birthday present."

Even though I had been friends with Earl for years, I had never been inside his house. None of the other guys had either.

The back door had once been white, but now only a few islands of paint clung to the sun-bleached wood. Inside the kitchen, stacks of dirty dishes and pots leaned precariously from the counters. Flies prowled through the shadows. The stink of cat urine filled the air like stale incense as Earl led me down a gloomy hall. Outside, the sun glowed clean and clear, but in here it looked like permanent twilight.

Earl pointed. "I come home and this is what I find."

Earl always had a smirk on his face, like he knew something nobody else did. Now the mouth smiled, but the eyes flashed anger. "Go on," he said.

The living room was small. A sofa and two stuffed chairs peeked out from under an avalanche of yellowed newspapers. The room had a high ceiling with an ancient brass light fixture hung from the center.

A man hung from the light fixture.

I'd heard the expression but never believed it was possible until that moment: my heart stopped. I stared at the purple face of a skinny man I had never seen before. A second passed, then another. My knees melted. Colored lights danced at the edge of my vision and spread toward the center. I collapsed in a stack of newspapers older than me.

CHAPTER 11

When I opened my eyes, a man's face loomed close enough to make me gasp. A thin face with a narrow nose. Five o'clock shadow in the middle of the day. A faint whiff of Old Spice. Out of sight, someone said, "He'll be okay. Just fainted."

The guy's gray eyes scoured me like I was dinner. "You lead an interesting life," he said as he stood and brushed leaf fragments off the knees of his suit pants.

I sat up on the stretcher. Red and blue lights flashed all around Earl's house like the carnival was in town. Guys in blue coveralls packed gear into the back of an ambulance. Cops hunted through the underbrush around Earl's house with flashlights, even though it was daylight.

As my senses returned, I said, "Who are you?" He stood tall and his blue suit had creases so sharp they could have been used as weapons. He was roughly my father's age, but his hair was prematurely white. Not gray. White. Like not even a molecule of color remained in his scalp.

"Detective Lieutenant Munson. I just had the Janey Young case dropped in my lap. And I understand you're the bright little fellow who found her."

"I'm no bright little fellow. My name's Jake and I'm not a little kid."

"Sorry, just thought after being unconscious you might want to take it easy."

"Where's Earl?" I said.

"How well do you know Earl?"

"For years. Where is he?"

"He'll be at the hospital for a while. Did he and his father get along?"

"I don't know."

An eyebrow went up. Munson didn't even have to say to cut the crap.

"Detective, I swear to God, I've never gone into Earl's house before today. I never met his father."

"He ever talk about him?"

"No."

"You ever think that was strange?"

"Earl's strange. You just accept him like he is."

"Strange how?"

"You know. Quiet. Kinda keeps to himself. But when he says something, it's so drop-dead funny, you want to shit yourself."

Munson's lips compressed. "Yeah, I got a captain like that."

"Funny?"

Munson shook his head. "No, makes me want to shit myself. C'mon, I'll drive you home."

Even though his car was unmarked, it smelled like a police car. I had known the privilege of riding in a few police cars in my brief life. They all smelled the same. A thousand brands of sweat and cigarettes mixed with greasy food and fear. I had borrowed one of my dad's Mickey Spillane novels and that's how I thought Mike Hammer would describe it. I was a slave to whatever author I was reading. For the present, my world was dominated by *I, The Jury.*

Munson asked, "Did Earl know the Youngs?"

I pondered that. "I don't think so. Earl was quiet, but even he would have bragged if he knew Janey or Sharon. He never mentioned them."

"You ever see Janey Young near Earl's house?"

I squinted hard at Munson. "What're you getting at?"

"Nothing. Just covering the bases."

I thought for a few seconds, connecting dots the way I thought Mike Hammer would. "Wait. You think Earl's father had a big reason to kill himself. Like maybe he felt guilty about killing Janey Young? He croaks himself within the same week she dies? Isn't that what you're really getting at? A real easy solution?"

He stared at me like I had just popped out of the ground. "Kid, you're too much."

"I thought I was just a bright little fellow."

He chuckled. "You'd make a good cop. You pick up the angles right away. Come see me after you graduate."

"I can't wait that long. I want to do something right now."

"Why?"

"Because I found her body. I feel responsible. And her sister's my friend and I want to help her."

He stopped the car in front of my house. "Jake, listen to me. Janey Young could be a murder. That means somewhere around here there's a killer. If it wasn't Earl's father, you don't want to cross paths with whoever it is."

"If this was about Janey Young, why would Earl's father kill himself on Earl's birthday?"

"His birthday?"

"Yeah, you didn't know that?"

Munson chuckled. "Chalk one up for the kid."

"I'm no goddamn kid!" Oh, yeah. My big mouth again. Swearing around adults was bad enough, but swearing at a cop? I wondered if he had a length of rubber hose in the trunk. Could they really work you over and not leave any marks? But Munson acted like nothing happened.

"Look, until we find out exactly what happened to Janey Young, I want all you k...(he almost said "kids")... teenagers in this neighborhood to be careful.

This conversation wasn't going the way I wanted, so I changed the subject. "Why was his face purple?"

"You don't need to know stuff like that."

"Puhleeease."

He chuckled. "You've seen your share of corpses this week, haven't you?"

"Yeah, so tell me."

"You'll have nightmares."

"I already have nightmares so tell me."

He let out a breath and ran his left hand over the white stubble of his crewcut. "Persistent bastard. Okay, you know what's supposed to happen with a hanging?"

"You croak."

"Yeah, but how you die is important. You drop, the rope snaps your neck, you die instantly. At least on paper that's how it's supposed to work. But if you don't drop far enough, or the knot is wrong, whatever, your neck doesn't break. Then you choke to death."

"He choked?"

"Yeah."

"How long?"

"Is a Chinaman's name," he said.

"Huh?"

"How long is a Chinaman's name."

"I don't know," I said.

"How-Long *is* a Chinaman's name. It's a statement, not a question." A smug smile crept across his face.

I got it finally. I gave him a look like I'd swallowed a cockroach. "Was that one big in the 1890s?"

"I'm not that old, Jake."

"Could fool me. So how long would it take for him to choke?"

"Couple minutes. That's why he was purple. His heart was still pumping blood to his head, the pressure builds up, but the blood can't leave the head because of the noose."

"His hands weren't tied. Why couldn't he pull up on the rope or grab the light fixture and get loose?"

"Can you lift your body weight with one arm?"

"No."

"That's what it would take because you need the other hand to loosen the noose."

"You mean he was just hanging there all that time waiting to die?"

"Oh, he wasn't just hanging around. He was kicking and struggling and doing anything he could to yank that rope off the light fixture. If he'd been heavier, the whole thing probably would have ripped out of the ceiling. Bad way to go."

"Is there a good way?"

"C'mon, I gotta talk to your parents."

CHAPTER 12
July 11, 1965

During the summer I often slept on the screened-in porch at the rear of our house, facing the lake. Hearing crickets and bullfrogs helped me sleep.

From a dream, something pulled me up toward consciousness. Half-asleep, I heard what I thought was a big moth batting against the screens. Stupid damn bug. I rolled over.

"Jake."

The moth tapping the screens was Sharon Young.

I crawled from the sofa bed and unlatched the screen door. The moon's rays bounced off the lake like a big spotlight and pulsed across the porch ceiling. Great. Plenty of light for Sharon to see me in my underwear. At least they were boxers and not Superman undies like my brother wore. Embarrassed, I hurried back to the sofa-bed and sat down.

"What's going on?" My blood pressure went crazy. From dead asleep to sitting in my underwear with Sharon Young in ten seconds. I needed more air.

The springs squeaked as she plopped down next to me. She wore an oversize T-shirt, her feet and legs bare.

"Jake, can I stay here?"

"Huh?"

"Please. I'll leave when it's light."

"Why are you even here?

She grew silent and pulled her feet under her.

How is it girls can do that? Make the whole bottom of their legs disappear like a cat? If I tried that, I'd break something.

She finally said, "Him."

"What happened?"

She looked down and her voice came out just above a whisper. "He came into my room. He was drunk. He, he wanted...you know. He wanted to do it."

"Oh." That's all I could think to say. This was way out of my league.

"I'm afraid to go back, Jake, until he's sober. Please, can I stay here?"

"Are you crazy? If my parents walk in…"

"I'll leave before they wake up. Please, I have nowhere else to go."

I felt her trembling through the mattress. Finally, I said, "Sure."

I slipped under the sheet. She hopped to the other side of the bed and did the same. I lay there for a few minutes wondering what I had gotten myself into. What if my mother checked on me? Or my little brother wandered in? He'd go squealing on me faster than The Flash.

"Jake, will you hold me?" She sounded like a five year old. I didn't know how to do this. I had never been in bed with a girl. Wearing only my underwear and being this close to her, I started to sweat. I scrunched toward her and set my left arm on her side with my hand on her shoulder. I didn't feel a bra strap under the T-shirt. I didn't really need to know that.

I laid on my right side with my right arm under me. Leaving it there would get painful, so I pushed it up over my head where it hung in space over the edge of the bed.

A scent of honey and sweat and something female wafted off her. She snuggled backward so that her spine pressed tight against my stomach. Her hair fluffed into my face. It smelled like peaches.

The only problem was that when I inhaled, her hair got sucked up my nose. It tickled and I almost sneezed half a dozen times. My face got hot from holding back sneezes. If I twisted my head upward I could breathe, but it was uncomfortable with my neck turned like that. After a few minutes, my right arm began to ache, suspended off the edge of the bed. I wanted to move, but I was afraid to disturb her. In bed with the most desired girl in high school. What was a little pain?

Finally, to get more comfortable, I tried to pull back my left arm, but she grabbed my hand, drew it all the way around her chest, and held it tight. I'm pretty sure my hand was against boob, but it was a short-lived pleasure because her shoulder pressed too hard into my upper arm and my pulse began throbbing just above the elbow. That arm would be asleep before I was.

In a few minutes, I felt more uncomfortable than ever in my life. Left arm asleep. Right arm suspended in space so that it felt as if fire ate at the shoulder joint. Having trouble breathing. Oh, this was going to be a super night. Why did people make such a big deal about sleeping together? It was torture.

She pressed the double globes of her ass back against me. I was pretty sure she wasn't wearing panties. No bra, no panties, just a thin layer of cotton between her body and me. I was falling straight into hell.

Oh, God help me, her bottom pressed right there. How could it be both soft and firm at the same time? And warm. No, not warm. It felt like someone had dropped smoldering embers onto my mattress.

Destruction loomed. I didn't want it to happen, but my little equipment had ambitions. Oh, great, did she think I carried a roll of quarters in my shorts? Well, maybe a roll of nickels. Surely, she could feel it. I flamed with embarrassment. I imagined dead puppies. That was supposed to work. It didn't. She would think I was the worst kind of pervert. But she didn't move away. Her breathing remained steady. Maybe she never noticed. That felt even more crushing.

Somehow, after a million years I managed to fall asleep. When I woke up near dawn, I was alone. Had Sharon's visit ever happened or had I dreamed it?

Yet my pillow smelled like peaches.

CHAPTER 13
July 13, 1965

Nobody wanted to boat up to the head of the lake after I found Janey Young's body. Even fishing ceased. People feared hooking into another corpse. Except for Kendall, who was out on the lake every night, alone, supposedly going for catfish. But you don't troll to catch catfish and you don't use a six-inch grappling hook.

Eddie and I suspected that if Kendall snagged a body, it would wind up in his basement and the school's chemistry lab would experience a break-in. You can't just walk into the supermarket and buy formaldehyde.

Swimming diminished, even though it was now the middle of summer. The public beaches overflowed with people, but few ventured into the water. For days after Janey Young's death got splashed across the headlines, I heard sporadic screaming in the distance. Young girls showing off by wading in the shallows flipped into hysterics because a leg brushed against a submerged towel or a foot squished into a clay pocket on the bottom.

Friends flocked around the girls for a few minutes to get the details and the beach snack bars would do brisk business as everyone calmed their nerves with ice cream waffles or milkshakes. Food, the antidote for fear.

I wanted my life back to normal. My swampy domain at the head of the lake was where I needed to be. Nobody ventured into such spooky surroundings now. Perfect.

In the middle of the blistering afternoon it was too hot to get there by land. I loaded my tackle box and fishing pole and rowed slowly along the shady side of the lake. With only me in my flat-bottomed boat, it drafted not more than two inches. Alone, I could get *Crater Face* into places where others would run aground.

I pushed through a screen of cattails into a deep pool that backed onto one of the red sandstone cliff faces that rose thirty feet at an angle over the water. Centuries of erosion had eaten into the base of the cliff so that the shore along this stretch had a rock canopy. From the base of the cliff an ancient swamp maple jutted out over the water about ten feet before the trunk curved upward and spread into branches. That trunk was two feet wide, a perfect place to while away the afternoon.

I had never shown even my best friends this little fortress of solitude. I pulled my boat up onto the narrow shore and climbed out onto the maple trunk with my pole. Where the horizontal trunk curved sharply upward, I sat down and cast my spinner out to the edge of the shade. That's where the big pike sat, looking outward toward the bright water, waiting for smaller fish to pass. They lurked invisible in the shadows and swooped out before their prey knew what hit them.

My lure landed in the sunny water and I jerked it toward the shade. Shadows darted under the surface, but nothing hit my lure. I cast again. It didn't really matter if I caught anything. Fishing doesn't require results. It's the doing that counts.

Off to my left, one of the Great Blue Herons patrolled the shallows. Behind it, three chicks bounced against each other on the sand. They had most of their feathers, but they wouldn't be on their own for the rest of the summer. The big heron stabbed her black beak into the water and came up with a sunfish. She took it to the chicks who pecked and pulled at the little rainbow until there was nothing left.

If it weren't for the breeze, my eyes would not have been drawn by movement just above eye level. A beam of light stuttered through the leaf canopy and illuminated two strands fluttering against the maple's gray bark. I leaned closer. They looked like horse hairs, long, black, and shiny. They stuck to the bark with a bit of something brown.

My fishing line almost yanked me out of the tree. A green-gray head the size of my fist broke the surface and a powerful body thrashed the dark green water to white froth.

This was no pike. I had hooked into a behemoth fish. No way I could pull this thing out of the water without breaking my line. I crawled off the tree and over to *Crater Face* where I had a fish net. After reeling in the line, I positioned my net alongside the boat, dragged the fighting fish along the surface, scooped him up, and flopped him onto the front seat. The aluminum shuddered like tom-

toms from the pounding of his tail. This baby was huge, a largemouth bass. If only Eddie could see it, he'd die from envy. And I did it without one of his fancy lures.

The fish struggled in the blinding sun as I worked my hook from the corner of his mouth. The old timers always told me fish can't feel pain in their jaws, but I never believed them. How can a sharp piece of steel not hurt? If it doesn't hurt, why do fish go nuts when they're hooked?

I didn't have the heart to stick a knife in this guy. Or maybe I just couldn't stomach the idea of cleaning up fish guts on a scalding day, no matter how much I wanted to lord it over Eddie with my cheapo-lure catch. Cupping my hands under him, I tossed the big bass overboard. Fish-smelly slime covered my hands and the weight of him stayed in my muscles for several seconds.

After rinsing my hands in the shallows, I stowed my pole. I wanted to stretch out on the maple and daydream. As I climbed back out there I remembered the hairs which the fish had temporarily wiped from my mind. Now I hunched over and examined them with my eyes only inches away.

The little piece of something that attached the hairs to the bark had a dark reddish-brown color like fish guts. The bark on one side of the trunk was torn and the bright underlying wood peeked through.

Something had hit this trunk hard and left behind a piece of scalp and two black hairs. Janey Young had hair black as a crow.

I visualized Janey's body going off the cliff, speeding down, crunching into the maple trunk before pinwheeling into the water. The current here at the narrow head of the lake flowed slowly, but it could have pushed Janey Young's body out to the middle where I hooked into it.

My stomach rose into my throat. The fish almost got a free meal.

I remembered fishing near here the evening before I found Janey Young. Echoing in my mind was a scream I heard from the direction of these cliffs. I could still conjure up the sound of it mixed in with the squawks of the herons. I had convinced myself that the scream had been one of the birds, but now I wondered. If only I had investigated, right then, I might have seen something.

Jumping into *Crater Face* and hauling ass to the nearest phone seemed like an excellent idea. However, the hairs could blow away by the time I returned with the police. Could I touch evidence to save it? I knew from movies and TV that evidence was like holy relics in church. Only the priests of the inner sanctum, the detectives, had the proper blessings to touch them.

What had been breeze was now wind, piling up larger and larger waves across the water. Gun-metal gray clouds marched from the horizon toward the sun. These hairs wouldn't last the night.

Scurrying back to my boat, I opened my tackle kit and dug out a flat plastic box. I dropped the fish hooks it contained into the bottom of my tackle kit and climbed back onto the tree. I couldn't afford a mistake. This might be a one-chance situation. I sucked in a deep breath, let it out, tugged the double hairs free, and coiled them until they fit in the plastic box. I peered closely through the scratched plastic to make sure that part of the dried flesh was still attached.

Then I hauled ass to the nearest phone.

CHAPTER 14

In less than an hour detectives and uniformed officers crawled all over the cliff, the tree, and the surrounding woods like ants on a carcass. A scuba diver came up from the pike pool with a black-handled switchblade knife, still so shiny it couldn't have been in the water long. They sealed it in a plastic bag. Other guys in blue coveralls combed through the underbrush with flashlights. They looked like the *Science Patrol*, a cheapo, badly-dubbed Japanese TV show about monsters eating Tokyo that put my brother and me into hysterics.

After they had me re-enact how I found the hairs, they discarded me like a used tissue. Though it wasn't that late in the afternoon, charcoal clouds had rolled in and turned the landscape to twilight. No rain yet, but the temperature had dropped and thunder boomed in the distance.

Nothing could make me leave until I knew something. I hovered at the perimeter of the men in their blue cotton coveralls as they sifted through grass and leaves at the top of the cliff, going over each square inch of ground as if someone had lost a diamond ring. Flashlights flickered among the trees like fireflies.

They placed a yellow traffic cone back about three feet from the cliff edge. I wondered what it meant. Nobody would tell me anything, but that just made it more of a challenge. I drifted into the shadows and sat under an elderberry bush. A car door slammed in the distance. A minute later Detective Munson appeared and approached one of the guys in coveralls. They had their backs to me, facing the area being combed.

Munson said, "When can I see it?" as he pulled a handkerchief out of his back pocket and wiped soil off the sides of his shiny black shoes.

"Couple minutes. As soon as they get done with that section of the grid. We go in, you take a look, and then we're taking a plaster impression."

Munson looked up. "Rain's gonna make a mess of this crime scene. Better work fast."

What had they found? I wanted to run right over to that cone.

Finally, one of the blue coverall guys signaled and Munson and the head guy followed a marked path to the cone. Munson leaned close to the ground, turning his head back and forth to see different angles, while the coverall guy kept a flashlight beam on the spot. He nodded, got up, brushed off the knees of his perfect gray suit, and the two of them strolled back toward me. I huddled low behind the greenery and held my breath.

"What do you make of it? Bike?" Munson said.

"No. The edges are too distinct. It wasn't a pneumatic tire. Had to be one of those solid rubber ones. Flat surface, sharp edges on the sides. Like on a tricycle."

"Or a wagon."

A uniformed cop stomped through the leaves from my left. Great, Tony Rubino. I flattened to the forest carpet and prayed. If he saw me, a second body might go over that cliff.

Rubino said, "I hear you got something."

"Maybe," said Munson.

"What kind of tracks?"

"Maybe a wagon."

"Kid's wagon?" Rubino said. He rubbed his muscular neck. He wasn't fat, but he looked fat because he was so short and thick. Raccoon eyes. He looked like one of those football receivers with the dark slash marks on his cheeks, except with Rubino it didn't wash off. Maybe he never slept.

"We really don't know yet. Might have been a tricycle," Munson said.

"Nice way to dump a body. Off a tricycle?"

Munson snapped, "We won't know anything until the lab can look at the plaster cast."

Rubino swiveled around and almost caught me with my head up, straining to hear. "Where's that kid?"

"What kid?"

"You know, the little asshole who found the body."

"Don't know. I just got here."

"Don't you find it strange that kid is finding all the evidence? First the body, then the suicide, now the dump site? Think he owns a wagon?"

"What kid doesn't?"

"Hey, I'm just a lowly uniform cop, not a brilliant detective in a sharp suit. But you know some killers like to stay close to the crime, relive it. It gives 'em a thrill."

Munson scowled. "He's just a kid. You think he killed a girl who was bigger than him, hauled her dead body to this cliff, then a few days later hung a grown man from a light fixture? His name's not Lex Luthor."

"He's old enough to grow a dick and Janey Young looked better than a *Playboy* pin-up. Could be somethin' there. Teenage hormones gone wild."

"Sounds like a good headline for the *Enquirer*. Maybe you should call them."

"Yeah, like you got so many leads you can just ignore the kid." Rubino stalked off.

The guy in blue coveralls said, "What's eating him?"

Munson replied, "Everything. Guy's mad at the world. He's been trying to make detective grade for six years. When's he gonna get the hint?" He shook his head. "Look, anything conclusive on that switchblade? Was it used on the girl's eyes?"

"Need to get it in the lab to be sure, but the blade's the right size and shape. Gimme a day or two."

"Sure." Munson stumbled down the path to the beach and the blue coverall guy went back to the traffic cone.

The blue coverall guy shouted above the wind, "Let's get that tent set up." The light dropped fast as the clouds began spitting cold droplets. I stayed low and retreated into the woods to get home before I got soaked.

Until today I thought turtles had eaten Janey's eyes. Was the scream I heard two weeks ago Janey Young falling to her death? Or having her eyes gouged out?

I shivered all the way home and not from the rain. What kind of person cuts out a beautiful girl's eyes?

Somebody I didn't want to meet.

CHAPTER 15
July 14, 1965

"C'mon, Sharon, walk over to the window. That's it, that's it," Eddie whispered. His eyes focused on a second story window of the Young house.

We'd cut through some neighbors' yards on our way to Eddie's and he detoured us onto a knoll at the side of the Young house. We'd done this before. Lotsa times. But now that I knew Sharon, I felt creepy trying to peek in her window.

"Oh, yeah, take it off, baby. Now you need some air. It's hot up there. You need to come closer to the window." Any night we came or went from Eddie's house, we had to stop at this knoll while Eddie prayed for a holy vision at Sharon's window.

"Eddie, do you go to your window naked?" I said it as quietly as I could. No breeze stirred the night and I felt naked myself there on the grass, only twenty feet from the house. If the porch light came on, we'd be sitting ducks.

"Huh?"

"How many times have you sat out here? Have you *ever* once seen her naked?"

"No. But almost a coupla times."

"Then what are we doing out here?"

"I got faith, man. Someday it'll happen."

I didn't dare tell Eddie how Sharon had wanted to skinny-dip with me. I hadn't told anybody about spending time with her. Eddie would club me with a hammer if he knew I refused her offer.

The faint squeak of a screen door carried on the still air. A porch board groaned and my stomach felt like I had swallowed cold bacon grease.

"Eddie," I hissed, but he was already up and moving. That half second saved him and doomed me. Panic flight got me barely to the edge of the Youngs' yard when two tentacles of muscle plucked me off my feet and slammed me down into wet grass. A weight dropped onto my chest and squeezed the breath out of me like the dregs from a toothpaste tube.

"What're you little punks doin' out here?"

An answer barely scratched out of my throat. "Just cutting through the yard."

The punch slid off my cheekbone. I guess he couldn't see me too well. "You bag of puke. Don't lie to me. You was tryin' ta see my sister."

"No, no, she's my friend." I don't know why I blurted this out. How was betrayal going to make things better?

"Who the hell...?" Ralph's weight shifted and the snick of his Ronson cut loudly through the silence. A yellow flame almost singed my eyelashes. "Jake." He spat the word. The metal top of the lighter clanged, he closed it so hard.

Ralph dropped a punch like a sledgehammer onto my belly. My diaphragm locked up and that was the end of breathing.

The next punch drove my jaw sideways so far I heard a click inside my head. "You stay away from my sister, you creepy little bastard. You understand? You and your damn peeping-Tom buddies. Stay out of this yard, stay away from this house."

I felt his breath against my cheek. He spoke softly. "Lucky for you your friend got away. If nobody knew you were here, I'd do somethin' really horrible to you, Jake."

Eddie would be safe in his house by now. These were Serengeti rules. When a lion takes down a gazelle, the rest of the herd runs like hell. No way Eddie'd come back to help. No point in both of us getting beat up.

Suddenly Ralph was off me and his feet swished away through the grass. I lay there dizzy from lack of oxygen. Half a minute had passed since I had taken a breath. The dew from the grass seeped into the back of my shirt.

I didn't struggle. There's no way you can force your lungs to breathe after a hard punch to the diaphragm. You just have to wait while some little timer inside ticks off the seconds and says, okay, you can breathe again. I had vast experience in being socked in the guts.

I also spent so much time on and under water that I could go without air longer than most people.

Slowly, at first, I sucked in tiny gulps of air. A little more. The pain finally subsided enough that I knew I wouldn't pass out.

I felt like a traitor, a perverted traitor. Would Ralph tell his sister I was trying to see in her window? She might never talk to me again.

I stared at the coal black sky. Stars scattered across it like crystals from a salt shaker.

I cried wet wretched little sobs.

CHAPTER 16
July 15, 1965

A new, black Lincoln Continental purred up our driveway. I had not seen this car before, but a new car always meant Uncle Frank; none of our friends or other relatives could afford a new car. I hadn't seen Uncle Frank since he dropped off my fireworks in early June.

Big-ass grin, sunglasses, and teeth like a box of Chiclets, Uncle Frank was a tight ball of energy wrapped in gray sharkskin as he popped out of his car. Some guy I had never seen was with him.

"Ho, Jake, I want you to meet my man Fletcher." The Chiclets flashed.

"Is that the guy's first name or his last?" I said. Uncle Frank ignored me as he opened his rear door. I got suspicious when the guy pulled a big-ass camera out of the car. This guy was so thin he looked like a refugee from a concentration camp. His khaki pants and madras shirt flapped in the breeze like a flag. Was he getting oversized hand-me-downs from a sumo wrestler? His skin didn't see much daylight. Cadaver Man.

"What's up, Uncle Frank?"

"Fletcher wants to talk to ya for a minute."

"Why the camera?"

Before I knew what hit me, Cadaver Man was snapping off shots. He pulled out a spiral pad. He was so skeletal, I felt like I should go in the house and make him a sandwich.

"Okay, Jake, were you and the dead girl friends?" Fletcher asked.

"What?"

"What about boyfriends? Who'd she date? She was a real looker. Musta had a lot of guys chasin' after her."

"Uncle Frank, what exactly is going on here?"

"Fletcher's from the *Trentonian*. I promised him an exclusive. There's a couple bucks in it for you."

If it involved money, it involved Uncle Frank. He was like a comet of cash. "How much are *you* getting, Uncle Frank?"

"Just helpin' a buddy, that's all, Jake. Now answer the man's questions." He pulled out his wad, peeled off a ten, handed it to me. Whenever I passed through the comet's tail, some of the stardust fell on me.

It happened too fast. After they ambushed me, I wished I'd gone back into the house. The ten bucks made me lose my senses.

* * *

What had I been thinking? I got lightheaded the next day when I saw the morning paper. The headline said LITTLE SHERLOCK HELPS COPS. Under it on the right sat a photo. Of me. For a minute I just stared at the paper. Numb. Then I read the story. Then I read it again.

Across the street the neighbor's paper sat on the front porch like a steaming lump of dog crap. I thought of going over there and stealing it. Then go to the next house. And the next. Pick up every damn paper and burn them. My life was over.

I was suddenly capable of serious violence. If Uncle Frank had been there, I would have stuck a screwdriver between his ribs. And that little rag-bodied piece of crap reporter, Fletcher? Ditto for him.

I took the paper to my room and sat in the shadows. I didn't have to read it again. Every word was etched into my memory. How I found Janey's body; how I found where she had been dumped; and how the police were using me in the investigation. The reporter hinted that I had important information. What a crock, I thought. But selling papers isn't about accuracy.

Why not just paint a target on my forehead? I thought about that switchblade. And Janey's hollow eye sockets. Whoever killed her now knew my name.

CHAPTER 17
July 17, 1965

During summer vacation, I could never get enough comic books. Any spare cash I earned became radioactive in my pocket. I couldn't hold it for more than a day or two before I had to get to the corner store for a comic book fix, maybe an ice cream sandwich. If money was tight, I'd skip the ice cream and buy two comic books instead.

I took off on a comic book run, gunning my bike up a hill in low gear. As I reached the crest, I saw a police car ahead, in front of the Young house. Tony Rubino leaned on the porch rail. Buddy Young sat on a bench with his back against the wall. They seemed too relaxed for this to be business.

I pedaled past facing front, not wanting to make eye contact with Rubino. He said something to Buddy Young that I couldn't make out, his eyes on me the whole time. I pedaled faster, eager to get his X-ray vision off my back. These two knew each other? That could not be good news, if it was true.

The comics could wait. I turned the corner and hid behind a forsythia bush at the far edge of the Young property. The sounds of their voices drifted across the yard, but their exact words escaped me. I waited. Did Lieutenant Munson know Rubino was talking to one of Munson's suspects? What were they talking about?

I waited twenty minutes. Finally, Rubino got into his cop car and drove up the street toward me. I pushed into the forsythia bush. As he passed, I rotated around the bush, keeping it between us. Waiting until I didn't hear the car, I remounted my bike and glanced back at the Young house. Buddy Young leaned on the railing, stared right at me.

All I could think was, damn, damn as I pedaled away.

That night my parents went out to dinner. A little after ten, as I scouted the kitchen for baked goods and my brother glued his face to the TV in the living room, the phone rang. It was unusual to get a call so late. Reporters had stopped calling a week ago. I answered the kitchen phone on the third ring. "Hello."

The caller didn't say anything. I listened to static for several seconds. "Goddammit, Eddie, stop it!"

Was that breathing I heard faintly through the static? "Steve?"

I listened for half a minute, then got scared and hung up.

Minutes later, as I sniffed the contents of a rather dubious plastic bowl of green something, the phone rang again. This time I picked up the receiver, but didn't say anything. Silence at the other end matched mine. I heard breathing.

I had never hung up on anyone in my life. It just felt wrong to do. Rude. But I lowered the receiver onto the phone hook and stepped away like the phone might bite me.

I felt so scared, I had to remind my lungs to breathe again.

CHAPTER 18
July 18, 1965

"Faster, faster. Make believe a shark's chasing you."

My dad had slowed his stroke to give me advice, then hauled himself forward so fast, it was like I had lead weights on my shins. He climbed up on our dock and toweled off before I even reached the ladder. Holy Christmas, he was fast. I thought I was one of the speed demons of the lake, but my dad made me feel like a cripple.

It was crazy. His tall thin body didn't have *that* much more muscle than me. Where did the strength and speed come from?

I made a last flurry and grabbed the bottom rung of the ladder, dragged myself up onto our dock.

"Dad, we don't have sharks in the lake."

"You'll swim faster if you think we do."

"Is that how you go so fast?"

"Yeah, maybe so," He got that thousand-mile stare.

"What?" I said.

"Nothing."

"Aw, c'mon."

He squinted. "In the war."

That's all I needed. I'm fascinated by World War II, don't really know why. Maybe it's because my dad had been in battle the whole time and was now a part of history. I often thought about what a fluke that made my birth. If my father had been killed, he never would have met my mother, I would not exist. "So, what happened?" I said.

"Sure you want to know?"

He rarely talked about the war. I had to nag him to get anything out of him and then it was usually pretty bad, like the time half the bridge of his destroyer got blown away by a kamikaze. Dad found his best friend's body with a six foot bar of steel right through him. To get the metal out of his friend's guts he had to press his foot against the chest and pull as hard as he could. He said the wound made a sucking sound as the metal wrenched free. It was one of the reasons my dad would never buy a Japanese product.

I hunkered down on the dock and hung one leg over the side. "You can tell me. It can't be as bad as that kamikaze story."

Dad sat down next to me. "We were moored in Tongatapu."

"Where's that?"

"South Pacific. A little island chain like Tahiti. We'd been at sea about two months, so everybody wanted to get ashore, but you can't leave a warship without a crew. So, the skipper rotated out the three watches, three hours apiece. My watch got sent in first. Some guys got drunk, some guys chased the native women, and some gambled."

"You chase the women, Dad?"

"No, I didn't want to spend the next month scratchin' my balls. I played poker and won five hundred bucks. I'd always quit when I was ahead, so I got up to leave. Jonesy, one of my buddies, had lost all his money, so he and I headed back to the harbor.

"Tongatapu had a decent-sized harbor with maybe five or six other ships moored there. The water taxis were busy as hell moving sailors back and forth from the battleship and the cruisers. Our dinky little destroyer they didn't give two farts about. Jonesy and I decided to swim."

"In your clothes?"

"Why not? We were soaked in sweat anyway. We had fresh uniforms on the ship. So, we dove in. The ship was about three hundred yards away, an easy swim. The water felt warm and smooth as glass, with the stars and full moon reflecting up off the black surface. It seemed like we were swimming in the sky. The next watch crew waited along the rails for our guys to return so they could get ashore. Everybody saw us hit the water. They started cheering and egging us on. The betting started. Sailors'll bet on anything. They shouted like it was the Army-Navy game. So, Jonesy and I picked up the pace."

"Who won?" I said.

"Not so fast. We were maybe fifty yards from the ship when all the shouting stopped. I mean, those guys went silent. I heard one guy say, 'Uh, oh.' The shouting started up again, but different. These guys were in a panic. They were yelling 'shark' and pointing behind us.

"I glanced over my shoulder. The moon was almost full and you could see really well. I didn't know whether to shit or go blind. A big gray fin stuck out of the water, coming right for us. The bastard was maybe forty yards back. I took one second to look at Jonesy and yelled, 'Swim!' I ripped off my shoes and hit it hard. I pulled out ahead of Jonesy. Sailors on deck screamed like banshees.

I thought my heart would explode. I tore through that water like I've never swum before. Even with my clothes on, I was pulling away from Jonesy. He started screaming in total panic because he knew the shark would get to him first. I just kept hitting it.

"The guys on deck shouted down that it was a big one. They kept hollering to go faster.

"I looked back real quick; that dorsal fin kept closing the distance. No way I was going to let that bastard eat me. Better to die of a heart attack from trying too hard. I swam like a crazy man.

"Next thing I know, I smacked against the float at the bottom of the gangway. I don't remember pulling myself from the water. I was just suddenly on the float watching Jonesy churn through the moonlight.

"Now that I could stand up on the platform, I could see into the water. That shark was huge, twenty feet if it was an inch. And it was so close to Jonesy, I was sure he was a dead man.

"I shouted, 'Jonesy, if you wanna live, swim like hell!'

"Jonesy kicked up a froth. He practically skimmed across the water. As he got close, I grabbed his forearm and yanked him onto the landing platform.

"That Mako came so close I reached out and touched the dorsal fin as it sped by. It felt like sandpaper.

"Jonesy and I laid on the platform, puffing like steam engines. Guys ran down the gangplank. We sat up and Jonesy looked at me like he'd been hit in the head with a baseball bat.

"I said, 'Fifty bucks says I can beat you going back.'"

CHAPTER 19

From around a copse of trees that stuck out over the water, a head appeared. Short hair. Big eyes. Sharon. She waved. "Hi, Jake."

My dad said, "Friend of yours?"

"Yeah."

Sharon swam onto the shallows about twenty feet away, then stood, water at her waist.

"Jake, she looks like too much for you."

As she strode forward, Sharon raised her hands and sluiced them back across her face and hair to squeeze out the water. She stepped up onto the sand. She had the same white bikini. And the same body.

Dad whispered, "Hell, she looks like too much for *me*. You sure you know what you're doing?"

"Daaad."

He punched me in the shoulder, waved at Sharon and hiked up the hill to the house. Dad's philosophy: If it doesn't present imminent death it isn't worth worrying about.

Sharon covered the twenty feet with a gait that I couldn't help but stare at. Everything on her moved in such a coordinated way, like ballet. Never, in all the times I had seen her, did she seem awkward.

"Can I borrow your towel?"

She could borrow my internal organs on a silver plate, if she asked. But all I said was, "Sure."

She sat down next to me on the dock and covered her head with my towel, massaged it over her hair. When her face emerged, she was grinning with such pleasure, as if that towel was the softest thing in the universe. She ran it over her arms, over her breasts, across that flat stomach, down to the tips of her toes. I would trade my soul to be that towel.

"No friends today?" She scanned my yard. Her short hair spiked out in a million directions.

"Nah."

"No book?"

"Don't feel like reading."

"What's wrong? You seem down."

"Didn't you read the newspaper?"

A frown. "We don't get the paper."

I told her about the front page story.

"Sounds exciting. Why so glum?"

I couldn't tell her about the phone call from Munson and how he he'd ripped a new ass in my guts. He thought I'd blabbed.

"I can't go anywhere. Reporters want to talk to me. They think I'm helping the police."

"Are you?" She stared intently.

I had not lied to her. Yet. We had a pact to share our secrets. "Why would they want a kid to help them?" I said. Did that qualify as a lie? Maybe I'd grow up to be a politician.

"You found my sister and where she was thrown into the lake. You might have seen something you haven't remembered yet. Makes sense the police would stay in touch with you."

"In touch" would hardly describe the phone call I got from Munson after he saw the Little Sherlock article. After he reamed me, he made me swear not to repeat anything we discussed. I veered the conversation in a different direction. "Sharon, somebody killed your sister. If that person thinks I know something..." I didn't finish.

Her golden eyes engulfed me. "Did the police say who they thought that might be?"

"No. They'd never tell me something like that."

She continued to stare into my eyes as if nothing else existed. "But you have an idea, don't you?"

How could I tell her I suspected her father?

"Sharon, I, I... I'm worried about you."

A frown pulled at the perfect landscape of her face. "What do you mean?"

"Your father." I lowered my head. I couldn't look at her and say it. "He's a scary man."

She said nothing.

"I saw him burning a wagon in your back yard."

"So?"

"If I tell you something, you have to promise not to repeat it." I looked up.

She nodded.

"I heard the police talking at the cliff where Janey was dumped. Wagon tracks led up to the cliff edge, from a kid's wagon." For the first time, I saw creases on her forehead. I said, "Sharon, you might be in danger."

Her eyes broke contact with me. She glanced over her shoulder at the water. "I think you may be right."

CHAPTER 20

The hot fist of July night squashed us into the earth. The humidity hung so thick my underwear stuck to me. "Eddie, let's get some Popsicles. I can't take this heat."

I didn't have to twist Eddie's arm. "Yeah," he said.

We walked along the thick hedge separating Eddie's yard from the Youngs' yard. Through the hedge, we saw a flickering glow.

Eddie whispered, "What's that bastard doin'? He only burns trash during the day."

"Maybe he thinks it isn't hot enough tonight."

We crept up to the hedge. We had great expertise in creeping. It was our occupation. As we peered at the fire through a gap in the branches, Eddie turned toward me, held his nose, and scrunched up his face. What a killer stench. Burning rubber.

Flames licked around an old wooden wagon with high sides. They didn't make them like that anymore. We backed off and strolled out to the street.

Eddie said, "What the hell's that about?"

Should I tell Eddie about the wagon tracks the police found at the cliffs? I said, "Who knows? He's an asshole." Yeah, I had a future as a politician.

We strolled to the corner store. I bought an orange Popsicle and Eddie got some blue thing that tasted like whale vomit, as far as I was concerned. We had just torn off the wrappers and had started drifting back to Eddie's house when we heard a voice behind us.

"Hey, pukeface."

That could have been either of us, so we both turned around. We knew the voice. We began chomping on our Popsicles to get them down before we might have to run. In fact, it was a pretty sure bet that we would be running. The guy who shouted at us was Ralph Young and he didn't look happy.

"Not you, Birdbrain, the other dumb-ass pukeface. Little Sherlock." Ralph closed the gap rapidly.

I got brain freeze from swallowing too much Popsicle too fast.

Ralph wore a white T-shirt and jeans. It seemed all the guys who owned hot rods wore T-shirts and jeans. It was like they all agreed or something. The weird thing was the way all of them filled out their clothes. Ralph had muscles bulging all over the place. Why are some guys like that? I couldn't grow muscles to save my soul. I once spent two weeks lifting a ten-pound ingot of lead I found in the garage. Up, down, biceps, triceps, three times a day until my arms got so sore my fingers twitched, but I didn't grow a single muscle.

Ralph was nineteen, with a car and a job. He didn't just walk. He rolled from side to side. That was another thing that bugged me about a lot of these guys. They each had some damn walk. And I'm sure they bought their T-shirts two sizes too small, so they'd look even bulgier.

His muscular index finger poked into my chest like a saber. "You tryin' ta get my old man in trouble?"

"No."

"Then why you tellin' cops shit-ass lies about him?" Shadow obscured his face. A streetlight half a block away reflected off the oil slick of his pompadour.

"I'm not telling anybody anything. What the hell do I know?"

"You don't hav'ta know anything to make trouble. You want trouble, Sherlock?"

"No."

Not being the focus of the storm, Eddie slowly edged back from Ralph and to the side. Ralph ignored him. All I could think was *Don't leave me again, Eddie, please.*

"I don't believe you. Why you hangin' around with my sister? Spyin' on us? Tryin' to get inside information so you can talk to the papers again?"

"Some reporter made up all that stuff," I said.

"That wasn't your picture on the front page? You lyin' little punk. Okay, Sherlock, you got a choice." He hawked up a huge gob and spat on the sidewalk. "You can lick that up or I punch you in the mouth."

My dad always said that life was all about choices. Making the right ones was the trick. I couldn't see how either of my possible choices was the right one.

Eddie had been unnoticed as he slowly maneuvered farther and farther from Ralph. Eddie said, "Ralph, if he licks up your tasty little snack, I think it would be fair if he got to punch *you* in the mouth."

If it was possible to will someone dead, Eddie would have keeled over from the look Ralph gave him. But I saw what Eddie had done. He provided me a third choice. He was far enough away that Ralph couldn't grab him and he had just drawn Ralph's attention away from me. I didn't need prompting.

As Ralph turned toward Eddie, he said, "Sparrow, I'll deal with you in a minute."

Eddie provided all the distraction I needed. I spun and sprinted away from Ralph. Simultaneously, Eddie launched himself down the street and within seconds we were running in tandem.

"You little bitches..." Ralph thundered in pursuit.

Ralph had strength, but Eddie and I had the bodies of whippets. Ralph could easily stomp us to jelly, but you can't stomp what you can't catch. And we were not about to get caught.

Ralph launched a string of obscenities at our backs as we pulled away. Eddie glanced at me, grinning the way he always did when we got chased. "Eddie, don't," I hissed. He wanted to make me laugh. Then he would laugh. Then we would slow down. Then we would die.

This wasn't like when the stupid neighbors chased us for blowing up eggplants from their gardens. We laughed like idiots. It didn't matter if we got hysterical because no way some fat guy with a wife and three kids could catch us. Being chased was something we loved. But this was different. This was serious. Didn't Eddie see that?

We had pulled a hundred feet away from Ralph. He was too muscle-bound to catch us. And he smoked. Eddie jabbed me in the ribs as we passed under a streetlight. When I turned my head, he had that look again. Oh, hell. I started to laugh. He started to laugh.

This was us in the moment, doing what we loved: escaping from danger. We engineered things in our life so we could have this happen. We weren't thinking about afterwards, that Eddie lived next door to Ralph, that we would have to keep a low profile for days, maybe weeks. We would need cat-like alertness all the time. If Ralph could surprise us... Well, I didn't want to spend the rest of summer in the hospital.

None of that mattered in this moment. We were two happy little assholes brimming with life as we whipped around a corner and dove through a hedge. We circled a house and came out on the next block, jogged down a driveway and cut into an arm of the woods that took us down to a footpath along the lake shore. We knew every bolt hole, hiding place, and escape route within a square mile. We settled onto a large boulder that stuck out of the water.

When we stopped laughing, we both got quiet. Reality crept back into our heads. Eddie was first to speak. "He catches us after this, he'll shithammer us."

"Eddie, when was the last time anybody caught us?"

"Yeah, but if this guy does, gettin' away a million other times won't matter. He's a sick piece of work. Just like his old man."

We stared into the shadows. From somewhere the scent of honeysuckle wafted down the hill and mixed with the faint odor of rotting fish coming off the shore. The lake frequently provided such strange combinations.

Eddie's voice emerged quietly, almost a monotone, as he said, "Jake, one time *she* came to our back door, was like two in the morning, scared out of her mind. I mean her whole body was shakin' and she could barely talk."

"Sharon?"

"No. The dead one. Janey."

"What happened?"

"I wake up, her poundin' on the door. My room's right there, so I look out my window and I see her standin' under the porch light. I go into the kitchen and open the door and she piles into the house like the devil's chasin' her."

"When was this?"

"Middle of last winter. Which is weird because cold as it was, she's standin' there with almost nothin' on. Some kinda negligee that I could see right through. Man, what a rack."

"Can you forget about her rack for a minute? What the hell happened?"

"She's gaspin' like a fish on dry land and she keeps sayin' *he's* after her. We should hide her. Stuff like that."

"Her father?"

"She said 'he'. Who else would she mean? Old man Young had the two best lookin' girls on earth under his roof."

"She could have meant Ralph."

"Jake, who's tellin' this freakin' story?"

"Okay, what happened?"

"My mom comes into the kitchen. I'm thinkin' she'll have a stroke the way she looks at Janey, half-naked and all. She throws a robe on Janey and makes her sit down. She shoots me a look like I killed the Pope. I mean, I'm just lookin' at what's right there in front of me."

"Did her old man come to your house?"

"No. Janey stayed the night on the sofa and went home in the morning. I never heard any more about it."

"It only happened that one time?"

"Yeah, but there's always a fight going on over there. I swear I hear cryin' on their back porch sometimes at night."

"You think he poked 'em?"

"Janey for sure."

"How sure?"

"Pretty sure."

Living right next door, I figured Eddie would know.

I told Eddie how Sharon had turned up at my house, scared out of her wits last week.

"And she stayed with you on the porch? Jeez-O-Pete. What'd you do?"

"I slept. We just shared the bed." I omitted the part about holding Sharon. I didn't want Eddie to start getting crude about her.

"You just slept...that's all...with Sharon?"

"Yeah."

"With your clothes on or off?"

"Eddie, let it go. We have bigger problems."

"They can wait. What was she wearing?"

I had to nip this in the bud. "Eddie, she was afraid. Either her father or her brother was drunk and tried to rape her. I didn't see her naked, I didn't grope her, we had clothes on, and all we did was sleep. That was it. Now stop it!"

He pondered that. "Sounds like he's makin' a new move now that Janey's gone. Bastard thinks it's his own private Playboy Mansion."

"He has to be stopped."

"Stay away from those people."

"Why? Why can't I help her?"

"She's good to look at, Jake, but she's trash. The whole damn family's trash. There's nothin' but trouble gonna come out of that house."

CHAPTER 21
July 19, 1965

Johnny Blanco was the coolest kid I knew. He had a gift for telling stories that always ended with me laughing my guts up. And he had those dark movie star looks that made him a babe magnet. I'd see him in the hall at school with girls bunched around him like bees around a flower. Even when he was a lowly freshman, he could suck juniors and seniors into his orbit. He could talk to them forever about stupid crap like hairstyles and Hollywood. I never understood where he got all that garbage.

When I talked to a girl, I'd get through about thirty seconds and my mind would go blank. I'd get flustered, start to sweat. Not Johnny. He never got out of sorts. He always seemed to know exactly what he was doing, like he was an adult in a kid's body, but without all the rules.

If Johnny was matter, his brother, Georgie, was anti-matter. A year younger than us and about a foot shorter, I thought of him as a blond, blue-eyed demon. It was weird because I didn't know of any other blond Puerto Ricans. Different fathers, Johnny once said, and then he clammed up. It wasn't the kind of thing you got too nosy about.

As much as I liked Johnny, I despised his brother. He had no loyalty, no limits. He lived for excitement. He was like hot grease in a frying pan. Drop in some water and suddenly it sputters and spits and anyone nearby gets burnt.

Johnny and I slouched in front of his house, deep in discussion about what movies to see on the weekend. Johnny was as much a movie nut as me. Since the time we were old enough to ride the bus, we plotted movie expeditions. About once a month we could afford to trek into downtown Trenton to see a double feature. We'd buy these fantastic hoagies from Kresge's and camp in the Capital Theater all afternoon. If the movies were really good, we'd stay to see them again. We could burn up a whole day on these trips.

Johnny focused over my shoulder as we talked. He ran his fingers through his coal-black hair, my first warning he was nervous. "Oh, crap," he whispered. "Don't turn around. Ralph Young's coming toward us."

Crap was right. After Ralph chased Eddie and me last night, I had successfully avoided Sharon's older brother. I glanced over my left shoulder. Ralph recognized me. "Hey, pukeface." His boots hit the sidewalk like pistons. Johnny shook his head and said, "Here we go." I took off. Plenty of lead. No problem.

A bleached stick reached out from a bush along the sidewalk, tangled in my legs. I went down and tumbled hard on the concrete. Before I could stand, I was lifted to my feet by Ralph and spun around. "Where you think you're goin', pukeface?"

Georgie Blanco stood from behind the bush. He had a grin so big, I thought his jaw might crack. He waved the stick at me. Little bastard. He didn't care that I was his brother's friend. He wanted a show.

Johnny stalked up to him, wrenched the stick out of his brother's hands, and spat, "You little bat-brained turd."

Ralph pushed a brown lock of hair off his forehead, but it flopped right back down. His freckled face chopped itself into harsh lines. Muscles crawled around under his T-shirt like pythons. I knew it was hopeless to try to pull free.

So much power; so little control.

"Where's that pukeface kike, Eddie Sparrow?" Ralph said.

"I think he left town."

"Don't get wise with me, ya little turd. We got some settlin' up ta do." His left hand tightened its grip on my neck.

Ralph slammed a Mack truck into the middle of my chest. The wind went out of me like a punctured balloon. I would have fallen, but Ralph held me up. He hawked up a slimy ginder and spat on the sidewalk. "You still owe me for last night. Lick that up."

"Can't breathe," croaked out of me.

Ralph shook me like a dog with a rag. "I didn't tell ya ta breathe, I told ya ta lick that up."

My escape with Eddie had merely postponed the inevitable. I was destined to be here, fated to eat snot.

Ralph pushed me to my knees. "You're the lucky one, pukeface. When I get Sparrow, I'm gonna make him eat dog shit."

I twisted my head up and looked at Johnny. His eyes opened to the size of silver dollars. We both knew he could do nothing. Serengeti rules.

My face hung inches from the green and yellow blob that would be lunch. I struggled in Ralph's grasp, but I felt like a mouse fighting an anaconda.

Our little drama played out under a tall maple in front of Johnny's house. A sing-song voice drifted down out of the tree. "Hey, Ralphy. Oh, R-a-l-p-h-y." The voice belonged to Georgie. He was like a ferret. He could pop up anywhere.

"R-a-l-p-h-y-y-y-y," Georgie yodeled.

Who could resist looking up? I couldn't, Johnny couldn't. Neither could Ralph.

Ralph loosened his grip on me, craned his head back, his mouth half open. A sploogy, yellow mix of spit and snot splashed across his lips and into his mouth. Ralph doubled over and vomited what looked like spaghetti. He spat furiously, then dragged his left forearm across his mouth. Yeah, Ralph wanted me to eat a snot burger, but he couldn't handle one himself.

Georgie's maniacal laugh rang from up in the tree. That laugh was enough to make anyone want to kill him and Ralph seemed willing to oblige. He didn't say anything as he peered up into the tree, trying to locate Georgie. Another blob landed on his forehead.

If Ralph had been a nuclear reactor, all of us would have been vaporized in that instant. I have never seen a face turn that shade of red. Veins stuck out like blue worms crawling across his forehead and down his temples. He grabbed at the lowest limb of the tree and pulled himself up as if he were weightless.

Crouching, I tried to catch my breath. All Ralph's attention focused on Johnny's brother. Had Georgie done this to help me? I doubted it. In his quest for excitement, the cost to himself or someone else never seemed a factor. He didn't understand cause and effect. Or he didn't care.

Georgie's hysterical laughter got louder the closer Ralph got to him, like a Geiger counter of death. My neck ached from leaning my head so far back, but I wouldn't miss this for a case of cherry bombs. I could breathe now and my strength returned. I stood.

Georgie scrambled higher through the branches until he was at the top of the tree, about fifty feet off the ground. Much lighter than Ralph, Georgie could perch on limbs that would crack under Ralph's weight. Ralph climbed as close as he could, only five feet from Georgie, but his limb bent precariously.

Georgie's laugh got wilder. Ralph roared, "C'mere ya little spic. The longer this takes, the worse it's gonna be for ya."

With me, it had been business. Ralph needed to punish me, show he was boss, but he hadn't really been that worked up. But with Georgie? Oh, Lord, if someone offered me ten million dollars at that moment to switch places with Georgie, I would have laughed until I was unconscious.

Georgie hawked up another slime ball and let fly. Ralph tried to dodge it and fell off his perch. He grabbed onto a limb with one hand and dangled for a few seconds. Georgie's laughter took on lunatic intensity. He sounded like the entire monkey house at the zoo. He was having fun, more fun than usual. In Georgie's universe, he had achieved the pinnacle of experience, taunting someone until they were as crazy as he was.

Ralph righted himself and pulled up to the highest branch he could stand on. Reaching up to the base of the branch Georgie was on, Ralph let all his weight hang from his hands. Georgie's branch bent lower and lower. Ralph jumped up and down so the branch shook.

Georgie lost his grip. He smacked into a limb halfway down and cart wheeled. Next he crunched into one of the big lower limbs five feet off the ground. He oozed off the limb like Silly Putty and plopped to the dirt.

It took Ralph five seconds to fly down that tree. A fraction of a second after his boots hit the ground, his fists swarmed over Georgie, smashing a left, then a right, into Georgie's guts. Georgie laughed. Ralph punched him in the side of the face, first left, then right. Georgie laughed.

Ralph squatted on Georgie's chest and pummeled his face. On and on he punched until blood fountained from Georgie's nose. Georgie's cheeks ripped open like wet newspaper. His lips burst like cherries. It was like watching a machine slam caps onto bottles, or stamp car parts out of sheet metal. It just went on, each punch making exactly the same sound, delivered at exactly the same interval.

Through it all, Georgie laughed, a high hysterical shriek. If he just shut up, Ralph might have stopped, but he didn't. Maybe he couldn't feel pain. Or he welcomed it. He seemed to thrive on any extreme sensation.

Ralph hammered Georgie for about five years. Maybe Georgie was unconscious, because he finally shut up. Ralph grunted like a pig when he stopped, worn out.

Johnny and I just stood there. We had never seen anything like this. I suppose we could have helped Georgie, but that meant Ralph would have worked us over too. And in my case, after the little bastard tripped me, I wouldn't piss on Georgie if he was on fire.

Ralph stood up and staggered around. He looked at us for a second, but it was like we didn't register any more than a tree or a car. The way he was breathing, I was afraid he'd use up all the oxygen on this side of the planet. He almost stumbled as he stepped away.

Georgie lay inert except for the blood oozing down his cheeks, the dictionary definition of being lumped up, with a face that resembled the surface of a potato. By this time, even I felt a little sympathy for him. I had never seen anyone get stomped like this.

Georgie started laughing again.

Ralph turned. His forehead grew furrows. He couldn't believe it. I couldn't believe it. Johnny looked at me like we had just seen Martians.

Ralph staggered over to Georgie and kicked him so hard in the side, Georgie stopped breathing. I knew that feeling. Diaphragm lock-up.

Then Georgie laughed a weak sickly laugh, with the small amount of air he could squeeze in and out of his lungs. Though beaten, he wouldn't let Ralph win.

His brother finally yelled, "George, shut up! Just shut the hell up!"

Maybe coming from Johnny, it had some effect, because Georgie went silent. Ralph stared at him for a few seconds and shuffled off down the sidewalk. He didn't even bother to wipe Georgie's blood off his knuckles.

When Ralph got fifty feet away, Georgie recovered some of his wind and croaked, "How'd you like that snot, Ralphie? Salty enough? I got more for you." He laughed like someone tickled him.

Ralph stopped, but didn't turn around. He stood motionless with his head down.

If Georgie didn't shut up, he was going to be dead meat. Then it dawned on me that Ralph hadn't finished with me. In Ralph's current mood, I could be dead meat too. Ralph started turning back toward us.

I got the hell out of there.

I sat under the maple that curved out over our beach and watched the lowering sun turn the lake to molten brass. In a few minutes I expected my mother to call me up to the house for dinner. Somewhere off across the water I heard Petula Clark singing her big hit, *Downtown*. More British garbage. Whatever happened to rock and roll?

I absently touched my cheekbone where Ralph had slugged me a few nights earlier when he caught Eddie and me in his yard. The swelling went down by the next day, but I still had soreness on the bone. My chest was a different story. The smash Ralph delivered yesterday at Johnny's made it difficult to take a deep breath. I was careful to keep a shirt on when my parents were home so they wouldn't ask questions about the four blue knuckle marks on my sternum.

I couldn't mention anything to my parents. If they raised hell about me getting beat up, it would only make matters worse. I'd get beat up again. Probably by Ralph, then by complete strangers who would think I was a little skank for ratting out Ralph.

Georgie's parents never knew that Ralph had given a massive beating to their son. Johnny told his parents Georgie fell out of the tree. History was revised and Ralph became the Invisible Man.

I heard footsteps and turned around. Lieutenant Munson hiked down the hill.

"Hi, Sherlock."

"Oh, c'mon. I told you that reporter made stuff up."

"I know. You're in the clear. Sorry about chewing you out. I'm just curious how you got sandbagged like that."

I told him about Uncle Frank. He said, "We all have a relative like that. Don't let it get you down. You didn't do anything wrong."

"Yeah, well, I hope you're bringing me good news. You caught the murderer?"

He laughed and scanned the ground, a little unsure of himself.

"Here." I tossed him my towel. "Wouldn't want grass stains on that James Bond suit."

"How old are you?"

"You know how old I am."

"Yeah, well, sometimes I have to remind myself you're fourteen, you're such a professional wise-ass. Look, I need your help." He spread my towel on the grass and sat down cross-legged. It seemed weird to sit like that all dressed up.

"Did you talk to my parents?"

"Yeah. Your father said I could arrest you and your brother any time I want. They need a vacation."

"Wonderful. What do you want?"

"First, whatever we talk about has to stay between us. I want you to find out just one thing, nothing else. Can you handle that?"

"You wouldn't have come out here if you didn't already know the answer."

"I'll say this again, it's between us. What I'm going to tell you, you don't tell your friends, your parents, or your priest. If this leaks, I'll know it was you and then when you're sixteen you can forget about getting a driving license."

"Gee, Lieutenant, my word's not good enough? You have to threaten me too?"

"Sorry, this is serious. We have a deal?"

"Yeah, tell me."

"Have you ever heard anything about Janey Young being pregnant?"

I didn't see that coming. "What? She was pregnant?"

His eyes bulged. "Keep your voice down. Sound travels far over water."

"Sorry. I never heard anything about that."

"I've talked to some kids who knew her, but I didn't get anywhere. Maybe you could ask around. You can ask people I can't. I'd like to know who the father was. Rumors, anything you might hear."

"What are you thinking, Lieutenant?"

"Just looking for an angle."

"You expect me to believe that?"

"Jake, I can't discuss the details with you."

"Why not?"

"I can't."

"Bull. You mean you won't. Listen, Lieutenant, why are you even talking to me? Huh? You know the answer. I found Janey's body. I found the hair that shows she went off the cliff. I was the first to see Earl Broward's father dead. And now I can ask about Janey Young's pregnancy in places you can't go. You didn't come to my house because you thought I was an idiot. So, stop treating me like one."

"Kid, you're not an idiot. You're a pain in the ass."

"Yeah, I practice. Now, tell me what's going on. How can I help if you don't tell me anything?"

He stared at the water. "I must be crazy."

"I can't dispute that."

He scowled at me. "Smartass. But I guess I should expect a hard time from you. Your father told me your IQ score."

"He said what? The guidance counselors told our parents never to tell us our IQ." I shook my head.

"Yeah, wanta know? It's way up there."

I did, but I didn't want to give Munson something to bargain with. I said, "No."

"He told me not to tell you."

"So, now you're not only breaking police rules, you're willing to break a deal with my father? Lieutenant, I've decided not to help you." But I grinned while I said it. As gruff as he was, I liked Munson.

He dragged the back of his left hand across his cheek. I was surprised his hand didn't bleed because it sounded like sandpaper. "Okay, we have two competing theories on this case. You swear you'll keep your mouth shut?"

"How many times do I have to tell you?"

"Okay, one theory is that Janey Young committed suicide when she found out she was pregnant. The other is that the baby's father killed her to avoid embarrassment. Maybe he was married. Or just some mixed-up kid who saw his life sliding into the toilet and decided to fix the problem fast."

"She didn't commit suicide."

"And how do you know this?"

"Believe me, Lieutenant."

"Okay, for the sake of argument, someone killed her."

103

I squinted. "You still think Earl's father did it? Then killed himself in remorse?"

He shrugged. "It's possible. The timing is damned coincidental."

"You're wasting your time. There's a much better theory." I raised my eyebrows. I intended to squeeze his ego on this one. I made him wait.

"Do I have to beg?"

"A little groveling would be nice."

Munson opened his jacket and showed me the shoulder holster, rested his hand on the butt of the revolver. The leather creaked. "Kid, I'm gonna stick this gun up your ass."

I laughed. "Police brutality now?" My face stopped smiling. "How close have you looked at old man Young?"

"Family members are always suspects. Nothing jumps out."

"Okay, now I have to get *your* word on something. I cannot tell you who told me this and you have to promise not to get all crazy trying to find out."

"I know I'll regret this, but go ahead."

"Someone tried to rape her. Janey said 'he' was after her. She could have meant old man Young or her brother, Ralph. I heard the whole story and I know it's true. If 'he' tried once, 'he' probably tried again, so whoever 'he' is, 'he' might be the one who got her pregnant."

That rocked him. Munson's lips pressed together and his eyes slipped into one of those thousand-mile stares my dad got.

"Or 'he' could be some other man," Munson said.

"Yeah."

"Like Earl Broward's father." Munson's eyes squinted.

"Not in the middle of the night at her own house."

"Got me there." Munson pursed his lips. "More motive." He stared into the distance for a while. "Who told you this?"

"I told you before I told you that I can't tell you."

"How long ago?"

"Middle of winter."

"Ah, dammit!"

"Blows one of your theories, right?"

He shook his head in disgust. "Blows half a dozen."

"There's more," I said. "A few nights ago old man Young had a fire going at the back of his yard. He burned a wagon, you know, the kind every kid has."

His eyes zoomed in on me. "Why would you think that was significant?"

Dammit, he caught me. Some genius I was. "No point in lying. Up on the cliff I heard you and the Science Patrol guys talking about the tire tracks going to the edge. That they might be from a kid's wagon. That maybe that's how Janey got dumped."

"How the hell...?"

"I have skills, Lieutenant."

He grimaced.

"Lieutenant, there's something else."

"You're killin' me, kid."

"The day before I found Janey's body, I was in my boat near the cliffs."

Munson got real still.

"I heard a scream. I thought it was the herons 'cause they were flying around like something had disturbed them. I didn't give it much importance at the time, but after I found Janey's hairs at the base of the cliffs, I started to think about it. I think the wagon idea is bogus. If she was dead and somebody dumped her from a wagon, she wouldn't scream."

"What time was it?"

"Sunset."

"Did you see anybody?"

"Right before it happened, I thought I saw two people sitting on the cliffs. It could have been a shadow."

"How far were you?"

"Three, maybe four hundred yards. Too far to be sure I even saw anything."

"Why didn't you mention this before?"

"The herons were making a racket, so I wasn't sure if I was hearing them or something else."

He just stared at me.

I said, "It could have been something else. It might mean nothing."

"Jake, don't bullshit yourself. You're too much of a nosy-Parker to not check out something like that. Exactly, tell me exactly what happened."

No changing the subject this time. Munson had that damned detective look. "You know where the sandstone cliffs are?" He nodded. "I had been back there and was heading home. The sun was setting behind me and I was facing back at the cliffs while I rowed. They were orange and red and I was making believe I was on Mars with John Carter. I swear I saw something move at the top of the cliffs, but I was far away by then."

"You said you saw two people."

I scrunched my lips and tried to remember. "I like to go up there sometimes and watch the sunset. I just assumed that's what someone was doing, but the more I think about it, I really couldn't see anything definite. It could have been a dog."

"Then what happened?"

"There's this pair of Great Blue Herons nesting near the cliffs, way up in an oak tree. I heard loud squawks and the birds flew out of the tree."

"Was it the birds made the noise or something else?"

"I've heard them before. They're loud. I'm pretty sure it was them the first couple times." I squinted as if I could conjure that evening into the present. "Then I heard another scream. That's the one that worried me. It sounded like them, but then again it didn't."

"Jake, you're on the water all the time. Was it the birds or not?"

"I really don't know. If I was sure, I would have said something before this."

"That's it?"

I hesitated. "Look, Lieutenant, I'm really stretching on this one. I was looking over my shoulder to check my bearings. I wasn't looking at the cliffs when I heard it. I thought I might've heard a splash."

"What? Was there a splash or not?"

"I can't be sure. I looked for waves, but that stretch along the shore is so thick with reeds I couldn't see the water."

"So why didn't you go back? I can't imagine you'd let a mystery pass you by."

"I thought about it, but, like I said, the sun was setting and I was getting dive-bombed by like a million mosquitoes. My jerk of a brother stole the bug repellent I keep stashed in the boat, so I had to get off the water fast."

"Jake, I hope it was the birds. Because if it wasn't..." He got that stare again.

"What? What are you thinking?"

"If somebody was up there, they saw you. That shiny boat of yours would stick out like a sore thumb."

"So?"

"They might think you saw them too."

My mouth said, "You read too much Mickey Spillane," but suddenly I needed more air and I wasn't even running.

He shook his head. "I might have to start calling you Mister PITA."

"Huh?"

"Mister Pain-In-The-Ass."

"Yeah, but in a good way, right?"

He stood, picked up my towel, and tossed it at my face. "Kid, you are too much."

"Yeah, I practice."

He chuckled as he trudged up the hill.

I was in no mood to laugh.

CHAPTER 23
July 21, 1965

The next morning, Eddie called. "Get over here."

"What's up?"

"Your detective just showed up and Buddy Young ain't too happy."

"I'll be right there."

"Don't use the street or they'll see you. Come through the woods. I'll be in the back yard."

"Okay." I slammed down the phone.

I flew out the front door and ran up the street. Rather than head north toward Eddie's house, I ran east, into the woods. I looped around to the north and came out on the dead-end where Eddie lived.

Cutting through some back yards, I crept toward the hedge that separated Eddie's yard from the Young's. The hedge had grown a pair of bare feet. I slithered up next to Eddie.

He put his finger to his lips. Munson's voice came through the hedge. Whoa, they were only ten feet away. I thanked God that Eddie's hedge was thick or they would have seen us.

Munson and another detective fished through a pile of ashes with rakes. Old man Young stood off about fifteen feet, his right fist bunching and unclenching, but saying nothing. His left hand slapped some folded-up papers against his thigh.

"Where's the metal, Mr. Young?" It was Munson.

"What metal?"

"The frame and the wagon axles. The wheels."

"Ain't no such things."

"What were you burning back here?"

"Trash. I always burn my trash. Ask anybody. Been doin' it for years."

"We have a report you were burning a wagon."

"From who? That goddamn kid? What the hell kind of police force you got? You listen to a goddamn kid?"

"Why would you say that? Why would you think it was a kid who made the report?"

As if on cue, a police car pulled up on the dead-end street that bordered one side of the Young yard. Tony Rubino rolled out of the car and strolled over.

"What's goin' on here?"

"It's called an investigation, Rubino. We can handle it."

"Yeah, well I live three blocks away, so I kinda have an interest."

"Well, then go handle crowd control. Keep the gawkers away."

"There are no gawkers."

"Then get some coffee and sit in your squad car, but stay the hell away from here." Munson squinted at Young as Rubino skulked back to his car. It was pretty clear to me how Young had found out about the wagon tracks. I could save a lot of brain power if I just assumed that if anything bad happened anywhere, Rubino was at the center of it.

They poked around a couple minutes, then Munson opened a canvas bag and pulled out the biggest magnet I've ever seen. He dragged the big black chunk of metal around the ashes on a rope. When he pulled it up, it looked like a porcupine of nails and screws and metal slivers. The other detective stepped close and said, "Looks like a lot of crap."

Munson pulled debris off the magnet and dropped it on the ground. "Thank you for your cooperation, Mr. Young," he said. Munson and the other detective crossed the yard, got into their car, and drove off. As soon as they were out of sight, Rubino jumped out of his squad car. Young darted toward the street and met him halfway.

I whispered to Eddie, "What total crap. Young didn't tell 'em a damn thing. Mike Hammer would have pistol whipped him until he talked."

Eddie said, "Yeah, make sure you tell Munson that. Tell him how you watched him screw up."

Eddie and I crawled slowly along the hedge toward the street. We missed the first part of the conversation.

"That bastard kid's sendin' 'em over here. Everyone in the neighborhood thinks I done somethin'."

Rubino said, "He's gettin' to be a real pain in the ass."

110

"Ralph caught the little prick outside the house a few nights ago. Goddamn peeping-Tom. And he's tellin' that detective who-knows-what kinda crap."

Rubino said, "The kid's a troublemaker. It's all lies. Don't worry, Buddy. I'll clip his wings."

"Wring his neck while you're at it."

The screen door at the back of Eddie's house slapped against its frame. Two seconds later Duke pounced on Eddie, licking his face and scrabbling in the undergrowth, wanting to play.

Rubino said, "What the hell is...?" as his head and shoulders pushed through the hedge.

Our keen escape reflexes had already launched Eddie and me. We ripped around the corner of Eddie's house. Happy rumblings echoed out of Duke's throat as he nipped at Eddie's shorts. He thought it was a game.

Duke had no idea how serious this game had become.

CHAPTER 24
July 21, 1965

If any place in Lakeview could be considered our clubhouse, it was Kendall's. He lived across the cove from me in an ultra-modern ranch house. Having an architect as a father, Kendall was surrounded by all sorts of skylights and gadgets and stainless steel.

They had refrigerators everywhere - two in the kitchen and one in the den and one in Kendall's bedroom. The monster in the den was way bigger than the one my family had in our kitchen. And it had a lock on it. A big damn lock that Kendall said only his parents had the combination to. I can't count the hours Steve Lezar spent spinning that dial, trying to trip the tumblers. It made no sense. We had two big refrigerators filled with food, why worry about a third?

That was the difference between Steve and me. I ate food, Steve inhaled it. His waist expanded every week.

The weird thing is that for all the years I knew Kendall, I met his parents only twice. I never knew where these people were. If we asked Kendall, he'd say they weren't home, but he never said where they *were*.

We had two theories about this. Theory One, my concoction, was that Kendall's parents lived in another house. How could they possibly sleep under the same roof? Kendall raised poisonous tarantulas so he could feed them to his even more poisonous Gila monsters. Kendall was less than compulsive about keeping the lids of his terrariums secure. I never sat down anywhere in Kendall's house without first inspecting the area to make sure nothing was about to creep up on me.

Theory Two, which Eddie and Steve strongly favored, was that Kendall had killed his parents. For a long while, Eddie believed that their bodies had been weighted down in the deepest part of the lake, but lately Eddie speculated that Kendall had stuffed his parents into the big refrigerator in the den. That's why it was locked. "I mean, who locks a refrigerator?"

On slow afternoons, we invaded Kendall's father's study. He had every issue of *Playboy* ever printed. We had vast arguments about which bunny had the best ass or the best knockers. In the bookcase, we once found a copy of *Lady Chatterly's Lover*. A big blurb above the title proclaimed: Banned in England. That guaranteed we would read it.

We took turns scanning the pages, looking for good parts. The book was supposed to have actual sex, but we couldn't figure out a fraction of what was going on. That D.H. Lawrence was an obscure bastard. We wanted plumbing details; he gave us purple prose.

Whether Kendall's parents were dead or alive, the net result was that Kendall had an ungodly amount of time on his own. We loved it. We played music as loud as we wanted, we had plenty of food. We were totally, happily, wonderfully unsupervised, probably too much so. We were always hatching crazy schemes and running experiments at Kendall's, but last winter we truly lost our minds.

We made nitroglycerine.

I kid you not. We made honest-to-God nitro. Like some Manhattan Project geeks, Eddie, Steve, Johnny, Kendall, and I huddled in Kendall's basement and cooked a batch from a formula I had found in an old book at the library. The yield was about two ounces. I poured it gently into a pickle jar and we transported it out to a spot on the frozen lake a hundred feet from shore. We had waited until after ten to be sure nobody was on the ice. I set the jar on top of an overturned bucket and tied a string around the lid. Everyone else ran like hell to shore. I walked slowly, paying out the string until I reached the beach.

Eddie and Johnnie dragged one of Kendall's wooden picnic tables to the beach and pushed it onto its side to act as a blast shield. The temperature hovered near zero and our bonfire didn't help much unless you stood almost in it. We huddled behind the table so scared nobody wanted to pull the string and knock the jar off the bucket. Finally, Kendall said, "Aw, hell," and yanked the string. We heard a clunk. Nothing happened.

It's tough to sweat when you're freezing, but I accomplished it at that moment. Steve said, "Somebody has to go out there."

114

"And do what?" Eddie said.

"Well, set the damn thing off."

Eddie said, "Hey, Plumpmaster, why are we hiding here a hundred feet away if we could set it off up close? Take your fat ass out there if you think it's such a good idea."

I said, "We can't just leave it. What if some kid skates over it tomorrow and blows himself to pieces?"

Eddie said, "Suppose your freakin' formula didn't work? Suppose it's just a jarful of crap out there? Where did you get the formula, anyway?"

"From a science book," I said.

Eddie wouldn't let it go. "Do you really think they'd tell you how to make nitroglycerine? They leave stuff out of those books so kids like us don't blow up half the country."

I said, "Okay, Eddie, if that's a jarful of crap, go out there and smash it on the ice and prove me wrong."

Eddie stared out at the lake.

Johnny broke the silence. "I'll call my house. We'll get Georgie to do it."

I spent several seconds considering how the world would be a better place minus Georgie Blanco. Much as I'd like to see Johnny's brother splattered to smithereens, I had a better solution. Of course, it involved a cherry bomb.

"Johnny, got a cigarette?" Like I needed to ask.

"Sure." He pulled one out.

"Light it."

Eddie scowled. "What the hell you gonna do with a cigarette?"

I took the lit cigarette from Johnny and ripped off two thirds of the length. From my pocket I produced a cherry bomb. Before anybody could say anything, I shoved the fuse into the unlit end of the burning cigarette. This was now a time-delay fuse. I scurried onto the ice. In the silver moonlight, I easily found the bucket and the intact pickle jar on the ice. I set the cherry bomb beside the jar, picked up the bucket, and shuffled back to the beach.

"I figure we have about a minute 'til that butt burns down."

We retreated behind Kendall's picnic table, our eyes peeking over the edge.

"That's been a minute," Steve said.

"I said *about*."

I barely got out the words when the universe split open in a supernova. The flash was so bright it hurt the backs of my eyes. A giant fist smashed into the table and knocked all of us onto our asses. The noise echoed off surrounding hills for ten seconds. We shined flashlights out onto the ice and saw open water in a jagged hole ten feet wide.

Eddie whistled. "We definitely need to take this shit to school."

* * *

It was now a humid July night and Kendall's bonfire lit up his beach. It didn't matter that it was summer. We liked bonfires. We always had bonfires at Kendall's. If we got too hot, we'd jump in the lake for a minute. We lived like amphibians.

Eddie and I didn't hang around Eddie's house much these days after the run-ins with Ralph. We were fearful that the hedge would part suddenly and Ralph would rocket toward us. Kendall's was our safety zone.

When we arrived, Steve and Johnny just finished cooking three pike they'd caught that afternoon. All of us had some, snatching seared pieces of fish off the cooking grate with our fingers, then trying to swallow the pieces fast before they scalded our tongues.

Dessert was next. Actually, it was more like the main course, because three fish don't fill up five teenage boys. Kendall trudged down the hill from his house with what looked like a big pillow, but which was really a gigantic bag of marshmallows. It must have weighed fifty pounds. I have no idea where someone could buy such a thing, but at Kendall's the weird and the wonderful always popped up.

We jammed sticks into four or five marshmallows at a time - marshmallow kabobs - and held them in the flames until they caught fire, then blew them out when they blackened. Nothing better than charred marshmallows: crisp and burnt on the outside and sweet and soft on the inside.

Kendall's family had stuff I wouldn't even think of asking my parents about. Like right above the beach, they had a patio with an outdoor kitchen that was nicer than the one at my house. It had stainless steel counters and cabinets with brick foundations. A monster charcoal grill dominated one end of the kitchen. Another damn refrigerator sat next to the double sinks. Kendall had a portable record player plugged in on the counter. It had only one forty-five record on it that played over and over. *Duke of Earl*.

That song was the background music to our own private movie. Nobody knew all the words to that damn song, but at random moments, we all started singing the base line: "Duke, duke, duke, Duke of Earl..." Eventually, someone would be foolish enough to try a falsetto imitation of Gene Chandler on lead. Nobody ever got past the first few lines of the lyric before we'd all be rolling in the grass, laughing our guts up. Yet ten minutes or a half hour later, somebody else would break into falsetto and we'd scream until we hurt. It wasn't a proper evening until every one of us had made a fool of ourselves.

Kendall didn't own Beatles records. We hated the Beatles. They blew onto the scene like a hurricane and ruined our lives. I didn't know any guy who bought Beatles records. Why should we? Girls were insane for them and now treated us like we were chewing gum on their shoes. The Beatles had long hair; we had crewcuts and ducktails. The Beatles had British accents; we had crappy New Jersey accents. The Beatles had sharp suits with no collars and pointy Beatle-boots; we had cut-offs and T-shirts and Hawaiian shirts and flip-flops and sneakers. Overnight, we had become crap. So we hated them and all the other British jerk-offs they brought with them.

As I devoured my two-dozenth marshmallow and started to feel sick from all the sugar, I spied a flashlight beam cutting through the woods a hundred yards off.

"Hey, guys, what's that?" The light strobed through the trees, flickering, flickering, closer and closer. Soon it was in our faces.

"What's goin' on here?" Oh, great, the one and only Tony Rubino. Killjoy central.

"Human sacrifice," Eddie said.

"You have a permit for that fire?" Rubino growled.

Nobody answered. We'd never heard of such a thing. We'd had hundreds of fires at Kendall's. We'd almost blown up the whole goddamn cove last winter and now Rubino was giving us static over a lousy fire?

I didn't think Rubino really cared about the fire. He just wanted to bust our balls. He approached the boats tied to Kendall's dock.

Rubino held his flashlight beam on the side of *Crater Face*. "What's that?"

I strolled over to the dock.

"Why does your boat have bullet holes?"

"It was the getaway vehicle in a bank robbery."

"Don't smart off with me. You have a gun?"

"Well, Officer Rubino, if I did, why would I sit in my boat and shoot holes in it? It would be a very slow way to drown myself and anyway, I can swim."

In the backwash of his flashlight, I saw those pig eyes glaring out from their little black caves. Rubino pointed at a comet-shaped scorch mark that streaked across the aluminum. "What's that?"

"I don't know," I said.

"Ever play with Roman candles?"

Oh, God, was he one of the cops who had chased us? "You know, my little brother uses this boat a lot, Officer Rubino. More than me. You'd have to ask him." Yeah, I would put the cops onto a nine-year-old. Real brave. I was heading straight for a one-on-one with Satan.

Rubino stepped closer to me. In a low voice he said, "You been spyin' on me."

"You're misinformed."

"Don't give me that crap. You were hidin' in the bushes when I was talkin' to Buddy Young."

"I took a rest in the shade. No law against that."

"You got a wise mouth, kid. You better learn to keep it shut. You're gettin' innocent people in trouble."

"I don't know what you're talking about."

"You got that asshole Munson believin' your bullshit. But you're just causin' trouble. You don't know a damn thing."

I shouldn't have said anything, but my dad always told me that if someone got you down and they shit on you, you had to make them pay or they would think they could always shit on you. I remembered the conversation I had overheard where Munson had said Rubino was not able to make detective grade. I said, "Maybe you should let the real detectives handle the detecting."

Rubino parked that cop flashlight an inch from the tip of my nose. It was so bright I thought it would burn a hole to the back of my head. I couldn't see his face, which was probably a good thing, but I had no trouble hearing his voice.

"That lake has some really deep spots," he hissed so low only I could hear him. "You be careful now. Wouldn't want somethin' happenin' to you."

He laughed deep in his throat, then turned away. I didn't move.

As he passed my friends he said, "Put that goddamn fire out." He disappeared into the woods.

Kendall rose from the flat rock he used as a seat and threw several logs onto the fire. He loped across the lower lawn to a small shed that housed their lawn mower and tools, returned with a red kerosene can. He twisted off the cap and tossed kerosene onto the new logs. Flames leaped and roared. He did it again and again until the fresh logs caught fire and the flames leaped thirty feet high. He set down the can, speared a marshmallow on a stick, and thrust it into the flames.

As I approached the fire, Kendall gave me a fierce look. "Nobody pulls crap like that in my own back yard. Nobody."

Until that moment, I hadn't realized how much of a friend he was.

CHAPTER 25
July 22, 1965

"Are you sure about that wagon, Jake?" Even though he was at the other end of a phone line, I knew Munson was wearing his don't-even-try-to-lie-to-me-face. He had that tone.

"I saw it, Lieutenant, one of those old wooden wagons with the high sides. He burnt it with a bunch of other stuff. The tires too. I remember the stink of the rubber."

"Well, it's gone now. We poked all over that fire pit."

"Lieutenant, there's something between Buddy Young and Tony Rubino. I've seen Rubino over there more than once."

Munson exhaled. "Can't hurt to tell you they went to high school together. Played varsity football. They're old friends. Even went into the army together. Served in a Ranger unit in the South Pacific all through the war."

"Jesus-jumping-Christ." I was amazed how I got away with swearing with Munson. I wouldn't think of trying it with my parents.

"My sentiments exactly. Pretty clear Rubino is leaking information to his buddy."

"That explains it," I said.

"Explains what?"

I told him what Rubino said to me at Kendall's bonfire the previous night. Munson went quiet. His voice got low when he answered. "You're not exaggerating? About him threatening you?"

"No. He made it clear."

All Munson said was, "Dammit to hell."

I could hear static on the phone line. "Lieutenant?"

"Yeah."

"What if Rubino isn't interested in this just because Buddy Young is his friend?"

"Whaddaya mean?"

"Because he's Young's friend, he can come and go as he pleases, right?"

"So?"

"He had lots of access to Janey Young."

He groaned, "Ahhh, Jesus Christ goddamn you, kid." He muttered something I couldn't make out.

I pressed on. "Maybe that's why he hates me. He thinks I know something or I'll find out something about him and Janey. Maybe he's the father. Isn't it possible?"

"Ahh, kid, you're killin' me."

"Isn't it?"

I had to wait. "Yeah, it's possible. It's so obvious I just never thought of it."

"What would you do without me, Lieutenant?"

Munson sucked in a deep breath, let it out slowly. "Jake, I think maybe you should stay in your yard for the next five years."

I hung up the phone and stared at the wall.

CHAPTER 26

I wanted to see her. Didn't matter if we talked. Just a glimpse of her would do.

I waited until dark, figuring the people who wanted to catch me off my home turf wouldn't be out with torches and pitchforks combing the neighborhood. Not yet, anyway. And it's much easier to see into someone's house at night. Trying to look less recognizable, I pulled a baseball cap low on my forehead and rode my bike. I whipped past her house in a quick scout mission, waited up the street for a minute, then cruised by more slowly.

Lights burned from the living room, but I didn't see Sharon. No way would I try to look in her window from Eddie's peeping-Tom station. One experience with Ralph cured me of that. On my bike I had a better chance to get away if he showed up.

I wandered around the neighborhood for five minutes and passed her house again. Very slowly this time, in first gear.

After eight passes, I gave up.

I pedaled home and sat in my lab in the basement, not knowing what to do. I could call her, but if her father answered, he'd grill her about who had called. If she answered and her father was there, she wouldn't be able to talk freely. What if Ralph answered? He'd recognize my voice and probably come to my house and ambush me.

My hands worked without instruction from my brain as I pondered what to do next. With a mortar and pestle, they crushed sulphur crystals to powder, added sodium nitrate and charcoal. When I was idle, my hands just automatically made gunpowder.

I hadn't heard from Sharon. All kinds of things could be happening. All of them bad.

Being fourteen felt like prison.

CHAPTER 27
July 23, 1965

The next evening, Steve, Eddie, and I hiked part way around the lake to The Shack, a hovel of a place that made no other food but pizza. They didn't need to make anything else. The odor inside that place was so delicious it made you crazy-hungry even if you just had dinner. We stuck to the shoreline. I thought it was prudent to avoid the streets. I didn't want to run into old man Young. Or Rubino. Or Ralph. The list of people I needed to avoid was growing. Soon, I would need plastic surgery and a fake passport. That's how people disappeared on *The Man from U.N.C.L.E.*

My friends and I couldn't afford a whole tomato pie, though we could have eaten one. We each bought just a slice. It was the best pizza on earth, cooked in a wood-fired brick oven, plenty of fresh garlic and basil on it.

We perched on the curb outside, wolfing down our food.

A red Malibu swooped so close to the curb we had to pull our feet in as it passed.

A young woman piled out of the car – frizzy dark hair, chunky build, jeans and a black T-shirt – and stomped around the Malibu to stand over me. The first thing that hit me was a perfume cloud so dense my throat tightened in allergic shock. "You little punk," she screamed. The second thing that hit me was the spray of gravel her red sneaker launched into my face.

"What the hell...?" I dropped what was left of my pizza and stood up like springs had popped in my legs, backed onto the sidewalk. Eddie and Steve hopped up, but kept munching their pizza, happy to be spectators. Oh, hell, it was Angela Rubino, Tony's nineteen-year-old daughter. She came in at number two on my list of biggest pains in the ass I had ever met, just below her father.

"Why are you spying on my father?"

"I'm not spying on anybody."

"You little liar. You and your asshole friends are driving my father crazy. You're like a pack of weasels. Weasels with fireworks. My father's a good man."

Steve chimed in, "Your father's a dick."

That set her off. Not at Steve. She swiped at *me*. It was so unexpected, I didn't duck. Her meaty hand caught me full on the side of the face. I felt shock more than hurt. She swung a roundhouse right at me, this time with her fist closed. I stepped back and she missed, so she just started windmilling at me. She was a spoiled brat who, because of her cop father, thought she could get away with all sorts of crazy behavior.

I stepped back and instinctively got into a boxing stance. My dad's many hours of instruction took hold. I blocked Angela again and again. That first smack must have made her think I would be easy. Big surprise, Angie. She couldn't connect again. So, she did what she always did when she was frustrated. She went wild. Clawing, kicking. She became a Tasmanian Devil.

I turned and tried to walk away. She came after me. She pounded my back a few times, and I turned and blocked her again. "What's your problem?"

"You and your whole stinkin' family. I hate all you people. I hate your friends." Tiny flecks of spit flew out of her mouth with every other word. I wondered if she had rabies.

Eddie couldn't resist. "All that pent up frustration. Sounds like little Angie needs to get laid."

I turned for an instant. "Goddammit, Eddie, you're not helping!"

Eddie and Steve laughed so hard, they had to sit or they'd fall over. Eddie punched Steve in the arm gasping, "You're not helping."

Steve hit Eddie's arm and squealed, "No, *you're* not helping."

Angie changed tactics and began kicking at my knees. I'd wind up a cripple if she connected.

"Just stop it, Angela."

"Screw you, Jake."

"Don't make me hit you."

She reached down and picked up a fist-sized rock and threw it at my head. As I ducked she saw an opening. Like a dervish she came at me, all feet and hands, trying to scratch or punch, or hurt me in any way possible.

She had no intention of stopping. I had to end this. I feinted a jab, anchored my feet, and threw a right that sailed through her flailing arms and smashed into her nose. She thumped into a sitting position with the most amazed look on her face and sat perfectly still. Everything got silent. Blood gushed out of her nose.

Fighting with a girl is a no-win situation. Either she messes you up and you get called a sissy who couldn't even beat a girl; or you mess her up and you're a bully who beats up on girls. The fact that this was the daughter of Tony Rubino, the biggest prick on the police force, only made matters worse. Suddenly, my life circled the drain.

I just walked away. Whatever trouble was headed for me would know where to find me.

CHAPTER 28

"You did *what*?" My father lost it. If my friends hadn't been there, I would have wound up in the hospital.

"Jake's telling the truth, Mr. Johnson. She started it and she wouldn't stop. Jake took a lot of crap before he finally hit her," Eddie said.

To me, Dad said, "Her mother says you beat her up."

"Dad, what should I have done? I tried to leave and she attacked me from behind. She threw a rock at my head. She was totally nuts. I told her to stop or I'd hit her. She wouldn't stop."

Steve said, "Mr. Johnson, Jake threw one punch."

My father rounded on Steve. "Mrs. Rubino said you were making fun of Angie's weight, calling her a fat-ass. And you called her father a cocksucker."

"Oh, big surprise. Angie lied."

We told the whole story again, second by second. My father finally cooled down. "Alright. I believe you. Even you three con men couldn't make up all those details."

He sat down at the kitchen table, spent. "Well, Jake, this just adds to the shitstorm. You need to stay home for a few days. Maybe a few weeks. Maybe you should never go out again." It bothered me that Dad had come to the same conclusion as Lieutenant Munson.

"Dad, you think I could become a foreign exchange student? Go someplace like Brazil?"

"For the year?"

"No, for the rest of high school."

He shook his head. "Sorry, Charlie, I don't want to live every moment of every day fearing an international incident."

The sun had dropped below the horizon, so the red and blue flashers on the kitchen curtain caught our attention. Peeking out the window, I saw the bubblegum machine strobing on top of a police car. The doorbell rang. I hadn't thought it could get much worse, but I was learning that no matter how bad a situation was, it could always get worse. My dad pointed at me. "You stay right here. You don't move. Understand?" He pointed at Steve and Eddie. "That goes for you two as well. I don't need this getting further out of hand."

My dad sprang to the front door. We heard it open.

"Johnson, I want your kid," Rubino said.

"You're going to arrest him?"

"I'm takin' him downtown. Assault and battery."

"How about you cool down?"

"Are you gonna get him or do I have to arrest you too?"

"Tony, your daughter started it. She threw a rock at Jake's head. He has witnesses."

"His friends are liars."

"He tried to walk away, but she kept attacking him. Should he have stood there and let her scratch his eyes out?"

"He broke her nose, Goddammit."

"Tony, I'll have him apologize. He didn't want to hurt her, but she kept coming at him."

I bolted around the corner into the front hall. "I'm not apologizin' to anybody."

Bad move. My dad whipped around. "You get back in the kitchen." When I saw the storm in his eyes, I reversed direction.

"You get your ass over here, Jake," Tony shouted.

It was already ugly, but I had made it worse. Eddie and Steve stared at me like they wanted to melt into the floor.

"Tony, the kid's fourteen, a minor. Your daughter's nineteen, an adult. And she's bigger than him. How you think this would look in front of a judge?"

We heard the jingle of metal. "Turn around. I'm puttin' you in cuffs."

A moment of silence stretched into an infinity of silence. Eddie, Steve, and I stared at each other with our minds racing. Maybe we should run out the back, down to the lake. Take my boat and never return.

I barely heard what my father said next, his voice was so low, a voice I had never heard before. If he ever used it on me, I think I would have a heart attack. "Tony, you don't have a warrant and your daughter was in the wrong. You take one step into this house and I'll break your jaw. If you even think of drawing that gun, you'll be the one going downtown. In the back of an ambulance."

More silence. The seconds ticked by and I wanted to throw up. Eddie and Steve and I froze in place. I was dead. I knew it. My life was over.

Tony had been a tough-ass Ranger. My father was his own kind of war machine. These guys knew how to kill. They *had* killed. Oh, God, what kind of idiot was I to bring this mess to my own doorstep? I couldn't even imagine the staring match that was going on at the front door. Any second I expected a lightning bolt to sizzle off the front of the house.

We heard the hiss of the storm door closing. The front door thudded shut. The flashers stopped dancing on the window curtain.

My dad stalked into the kitchen and opened the cupboard above the refrigerator, pulled out the bottle of Johnny Walker Red. From another cupboard, he grabbed a shot glass. He filled it and threw the scotch back in one gulp. He filled the shot glass again and downed it just as fast as the first one. He took a deep breath and let it out slowly.

He set the shot glass onto the kitchen counter and stared through me as if I wasn't there.

CHAPTER 29

Following the unholy mess with Rubino's daughter, I retreated to the basement where my chemistry set and microscope stood in a corner on planks and sawhorses. I fiddled with some chemicals, made a purple mess that stunk like dead meat, and threw it all in the trash.

My clock said nine-fifteen. I heard my mother come home, heard her voice raised in response to my father. I knew what he was telling her. I expected her to storm down the stairs, but he must have stopped her. After a while the house got quiet.

Being on a hill allowed our house to have a walk-out basement, so, though I was exiled down here, I wasn't trapped. I shuffled out onto the patio and flopped into a beach chair.

Am I such a bad person? Okay, I have a big mouth, but why was I always feeling like the world was about to crash in on me? I remembered one winter in grade school when I had so much detention that I walked home in the dark almost every evening. I was in third grade and I thought I was worse than Hitler. Now, again, I felt like a criminal. And what had I really done but defend myself?

People had died. Cops were coming to my house. I was afraid to walk the streets. Was this any way to live?

The safe thing to do was follow Munson's advice. I should just stay home, watch TV, and let people forget me until I became anonymous again.

The problem was that I couldn't stand being inside. I needed to hike, and fish, and swim, and have adventures with my friends. Most importantly, I needed to be out of the house to avoid murdering my brother.

No, I realized I was just cooking up excuses. I felt crummy tonight because I wanted to see Sharon. I hurt so much inside that I needed relief. It would all feel better if I could see her, even for a minute. Yeah, I had it bad.

I convinced myself that my parents wouldn't notice if I went out. I was sure they wanted me to stew in the basement by myself anyway, so they wouldn't check on me. Probably. My feet just took me. First one street, then another.

Lakeview consisted of about twenty blocks laid out in a grid. Lakeview Boulevard ran north and south along the west side of the neighborhood and was the only street that connected to a main road. All the others just ran out of asphalt either at the lake in the south or in a wall of trees along the east and north sides of the village. You could step off asphalt and in fifty feet be in deep woods or deep water.

At a normal pace, I could walk from one end of Lakeview to the other in less than ten minutes. It took me five to get to Sharon's house. Once I got there, I didn't know what to do. I couldn't just knock on the front door. If her father answered the door, I'd puke. If Ralph answered, I'd probably die.

I walked past the front of the house. Ralph's jalopy and the old man's truck were not in the driveway. A red Corvette convertible with the top down sat next to the house.

All the windows were dark. I turned the corner so I could view the back of the building. No lights there either. Maybe I'm bold, maybe I'm stupid, but I crept into the yard and used the shadow of the hedge that bordered Eddie's yard to stay out of the moonlight. I passed to the far side of the house, rounded the corner, and took cover about thirty feet from the house. Sharon's window was dark. I heard voices. Giggles. Sharon. And a man's voice.

I slipped across the lawn to the rise where Eddie always tried to see Sharon naked. Her window remained dark. I waited a few minutes.

Suddenly, the windows of the first floor lit up, bathing me in light. If anyone looked out, they'd see me. I shot toward the front of the house where three butterfly bushes provided the closest cover. I could just step onto the street, start walking, act normal, but I wanted to see who owned the red 'Vette.

The car's engine thrummed to life. Headlights sprayed across the far side of the house and the damn car whipped around the front of the house and onto the street headed right for me. I scrunched down as powerful beams blasted through the butterfly bushes. The tires grabbed at the gravel and the car stopped. Triple damn.

"Hey, Jake, I see you."

I thought I would faint. I thought my skills were better than this.

"Don't make me come over there."

I knew the voice. I stepped from behind the bush.

"C'mere," he said.

I shuffled nearer, but kept enough distance that if I had to, I could run. From long experience I knew a guy in a car wouldn't chase too far and leave his machine in the middle of the street, particularly a brand new 'Vette. "What the hell you doin'?" he said.

In the backwash from the headlights, his teeth glowed. "Hi, Chaz."

"Why the hell you hidin' in Sharon's yard?" A smile plastered across his face. "You got a crush on her?"

I stared at my sneakers. My mind whirled. Chaz in the house with Sharon? In the dark? It was too much to absorb.

"You try'na peep in her window?" he said.

"I wouldn't do that." Thank God for the night because my blush felt like sunburn.

"Hell, I would. Every guy in the county would. That is one primo piece of ass. And so was her sister."

"Hey, Chaz, don't talk about her like that."

"Jake, c'mere, I ain't gonna bite ya." He leaned out the window, left biceps flattened against the door like a ham, box of Marlboros tucked in the sleeve of his T-shirt. I stepped up to the window. "There's two kinds of women in this world. One kind you marry and the other kind you just fuck. Remember that, Jake."

My stupid little world imploded. He had done the deed with Sharon.

"Whatsamatter, Jake? You never heard that word before?"

"I heard it."

"Know what it means?"

I gave him a sour look. "Yeah, it means you get horny and give a girl a tour of the backseat of your car."

Chaz laughed so hard I thought he would choke. He pulled a cigarette from behind his ear and popped it between his lips. The Ronson appeared. Sparks. Flame. Inhale. Definitely good way to prevent choking.

As he blew smoke out of his lungs, he said, "Let me tell you somethin', Jake, for when you get older. Girls like Janey and Sharon, you buy 'em a burger and a shake and you take 'em somewhere and you bang the hell out of 'em. That kind of girl is a certified member of the Four F Club."

"The what?"

"The Four F Club. Find 'em, Feel 'em, Fuck 'em, and Forget 'em."

He was enjoying this too much. I blurted out, "Why isn't she the kind you marry?"

"Who? Sharon? 'Cause every guy who sees her wants her. You couldn't watch her twenty-four hours a day. You'd never know if she was cheatin' on you. It would drive you crazy."

She was already driving me crazy and marriage was not even a possibility.

He grinned, his eyes gleaming in the backwash of the headlights. "Hop in. I'll give you a lift home."

"Naw, I'll walk." I had always admired Chaz, nuts as he was, but now I didn't want to be near him. He had been screwing Sharon just minutes ago and it didn't even seem to matter to him. My mind visualized Sharon all naked and sweaty and crazy and I bit into my cheek to stop myself from thinking about it until I tasted blood.

"You sure?" He flicked sparks onto the street.

"Where'd you get this piece of crap, Chaz?" I knuckled the fiberglass under the window. "I liked the Fairlane."

"Got lucky. My great-grandmother croaked. Left me some money."

"And you blew it on a car?"

"What else is money good for? C'mon. This bitch rides better than Sharon."

"Nah. I need the exercise."

"Suit yerself." He punched a cassette into his eight-track. *In the Still of the Night* drifted from the speakers. He barely touched the gas, but the rumble from the engine vibrated my guts. The Five Satins got drowned out by the eight cylinders. For ten seconds the night wasn't so still. His taillights grew smaller and disappeared over the hill.

I wished I had the nerve to go up to Sharon's door and ring the bell. Instead, I just trudged home.

As I lay in bed, not able to sleep, my mind made connections. If Chaz knew Sharon and Janey well enough to be screwing them, did he know anything about Janey's death? Was he involved in some way? Was he the father of Janey's child? I thought about the black-handled switchblade the police found in the water under the cliff where Janey had been thrown into the lake. What would happen if I asked Chaz to show me his knife?

I was driving myself crazy.

CHAPTER 30
July 24, 1965

The corner store may have had a name posted on its exterior, but its outer walls were so obscured by sheet-metal signs for Coke and Schlitz beer and Hershey bars that you had to be ancient to remember what was painted on the walls. We just called it the corner store. A sign that sat in the driveway lit up at night. It said: *Hot Dogs, Ice, Worms, Propane.*

The essentials of life.

What little paint could be seen through the layers of signs was cracked and bubbled. The missing shingles of the gray roof revealed a red roof underneath. It was a hovel, a one-story structure built in the 1800s. You could buy anything from motor oil to lunchmeat to comic books. The store had no organization, everything mashed together on the walls, on free-standing shelves, on wire racks. Salamis and flycatchers hung from the drooping slat ceiling.

Once a week or so, I trekked the half-mile to the corner store to stock up on comic books. In the summer, I knew nothing more pleasurable than laying in the grass reading Spider-Man, X-Men, or The Flash.

As I stepped around the corner to the entrance, I almost collided with Carl Hardwick and a guy we called "Animal." His real name was Billy Easterman. We never dared to call him Animal to his face. He was built like a bear and as stupid as sawdust. Animal and Carl lived in Lakeview, but I avoided them.

"Hey, Johnson, how's your little Johnson?" Hardwick leered. Echoes of the school shower room, where being the youngest in gym class, I was the least developed. "I can't figure out how your name is Johnson when you don't have one." Hardwick laughed at his own joke and cracked his knuckles.

His greasy Elvis hair shimmered in the sun. He had all the muscles of a hot-rod guy, but no hot-rod. And what a face. Covered with tiny acne holes, his face looked like it had caught fire and someone had put it out with an ice pick.

Crappy timing to be here. Open your door to trouble, even a crack, and it pushes right in. It flows like the tide and everywhere you turn, you get wet. Ever since I found Janey Young's body my life had been inundated by this tide. I marched to the store entrance without stopping.

"Jakie boy, you don't get away that easy." Hardwick stepped in my path. "Tell us."

"Tell you what?"

"Jakie, don't act stupid or I might mistake you for Billy. You know what I mean. Tell us about Sharon."

I put on a blank face.

"I got binoculars, Jake. I saw her on your beach. She was practically explodin' out of that bikini."

"It was no big deal."

"Maybe not for you, but did the little Johnson get some action? What was the angle of the dangle?"

"What?"

"Y'know. The angle of the dangle equals the heat of the meat times the mass of the ass."

I blushed. "It wasn't like that."

"Why not? Afraid? You got a gold mine sittin' right in front of you and Jakie Johnson don't got the balls to dig for the treasure? What a waste."

Animal leered at me and held his hands out like he was grasping something while he thrust his hips forward. "Yeah, pound her some meat. Hooyah."

I said, "Yeah, well, Carl, if it's so easy, maybe you can show us how."

Carl said, "You invitin' me to your house next time she's there?"

"No."

"You gettin' impolite there, Jakie?"

"I got things to do, *Carlie*." My heart ticked faster. I had strayed close to the line.

Carl turned to Animal. "See, Billy, he wants all the good meat for himself. He's not a friendly guy. He doesn't share."

Something in me snapped. "Meat? Sharon Young is nothing but meat?" A wave of nausea swept over me as I thought of the implications. "How about Sharon's sister, Janey? Was she meat too? You ever go to the cliffs, Carl? Maybe you and your pet monster tried to 'pound her

140

some meat' and when you were done you threw her off the cliffs so she couldn't squeal on you."

Carl was nothing great to see when he wasn't mad, but now with his thin lips pulled back and his eyes all crazy, he looked like something from a horror movie. I had gone way over the line. Before Carl could respond, I hurried to the store entrance.

As I opened the door, Carl sneered to Animal, "Hey, Billy, Jakie told me he could kick your stupid ass. Told me yesterday. Said you were a dumb ox and he'd like to pound on you 'til the snot came out of your nose. More snot than usual, he meant."

Billy's deep-set eyes fixed on me like I was his next meal. Goddamn Neanderthal. Carl kept on. "Yeah, he said he was glad he came up with the name Animal for you. Calls you that all the time behind your back. 'Big, dumb-ass Animal' he calls you. Ain't that right, Jakie?"

I stepped into the coolness of the old store and closed the door. Hardwick was a total jerk, but he'd never been this aggressive. His older brother had been a classmate of Ralph Young. Would Ralph have everybody he'd ever known gunning for me?

I took longer than usual picking out comic books, hoping the pair out front might get bored and scatter. But Big Bob, the owner, eyeballed me like I was trying to steal something, so I paid him. When I stepped out of the shadowy interior to the blinding light outside, I squinted. I almost didn't see Animal come for me. If I hadn't heard him grunting, he could have planted a meaty fist in the center of my face and sent me straight to Queersville. I barely ducked in time.

His next rush was a surprise. For him. I jabbed his face twice, real quick and stepped to the left. He reached halfway to China and lobbed a punch at me. I easily stepped aside and hit him with a quick left and a harder right. Billy's face blotched up. Fat and out of shape, he opened his mouth wide and breathed hard. Under his crewcut, his scalp turned red.

My initial fear diminished as I saw that Animal couldn't really get to me. I thanked my father for all those hours of boxing training. I peppered Animal's face and stayed out of range of his slow haymakers. I felt like I could do it all day.

From around the side of the store two of my friends appeared: Steve and Johnny. With them watching, I got cocky. I should have learned by now that when I get cocky I get stupid. I had just hammered Billy with a left hook that smooshed his fat nose across his fat face and produced a bright ribbon of blood. Now he really looked like an animal.

"C'mon, Animal. You want some more? I'll break your jaw next time. Then you're gonna swallow some teeth." Oh, I was full of myself. I could see how a guy might really get into fighting. I took a lot of crap from guys like Hardwick and Billy and being able to lump up Billy's face in front of my friends felt like heavenly justice.

There is no heaven and there is no justice. Billy lunged at me with his arms wide. For a second, all I could think was, hey, this is boxing, you can't do that. Nobody had explained to me that street fights don't have rules.

One of Billy's arms caught me around the waist and I stumbled onto the hot asphalt of the store's parking lot. I scrambled to escape, but I was a rabbit caught by a boa constrictor. Billy worked his way up my body, squeezing and pulling. Before I knew it, he wrapped his thick arms around my neck from behind. The last puff of air that made it into my nose carried the stale garlic of Animal's breath and the even more stale sweat of his body.

Breathing stopped. Panic started.

My sole purpose in life focused down to sucking air into a throat that Billy had clamped shut. My head throbbed, my eyes bulged. Big red splotches of light exploded at the edges of my vision, worked into the center. I wasn't faking when I went limp. Even then, Animal seemed oblivious to my lack of resistance. I think he would have clung to me until my body was cold.

But something happened. I heard a screech of tires and a door slam. I heard a thump and I could breathe again. I heard a yelp, then a groan. Then more scuffling sounds.

In slow motion, I rolled onto my side. Animal lay flat on his back. I watched Chaz hammer his fists into Animal like a baker punching dough. Whump, the fist hit and disappeared into the fat. Animal groaned. The other fist did the same. This went on until I think Chaz got bored. Finally, Chaz gripped both hands together and clubbed Animal on the left temple. Animal rolled onto his side and didn't move.

I was perfectly happy to stare at the robin's-egg sky for the rest of the day as sweet air trickled into my lungs. Chaz's face loomed into my vision. "C'mon, Jake. Get up."

I didn't recognize the croaking voice that said, "Lemme lay here."

Chaz lifted me to my feet. "Can you walk?"

I nodded. I was regaining strength, but my throat hurt like hell. As Chaz helped me to his car, I rasped, "My comic books," and pointed to the driveway.

"Are you nuts?" But he walked over and grabbed my stack of comics.

And that was it. Chaz helped me into his 'Vette, and dropped the damaged comic books onto my lap. Carl Hardwick stood over Animal's unmoving body like he didn't know what to do. Johnny and Steve hustled down the street before Hardwick could work off his frustration on them.

Chaz's V-8 torqued up and slammed me back into the seat harder than Animal had ever hit me. Having not been able to breathe, I now reveled in it. I sucked in the rich aroma of the black leather bucket seats.

"What the hell you doin' messin' with that retard?" Chaz said. He shifted to second and crushed me into the seat again. "You're more retarded than he is."

"*I'm* retarded?" I croaked.

Chaz shook his head and chuckled. "You're a nut case, Jake."

He threw the car into third and hit the gas. I swear I couldn't breathe for five seconds.

"Chaz, can I borrow your switchblade?"

"What for?"

"I have a hangnail."

"Jake, you're delirious."

"No, I'm serious."

"I lost it," he said.

I regretted asking.

CHAPTER 31
July 25, 1965

"Jake, phone," my mother shouted at me from the back porch.

I rarely got phone calls. My friends were either here or not here. Or I was at one of their houses. Or not there. We were existential. We didn't go in for chatting.

I trudged up the hill. As I got near the house my mother said, "Hurry, it's a girl."

Trotting through the basement entrance, I grabbed the wall phone just inside the door. "I got it, Mom." I heard the click as she hung up her extension. "Yeah?"

"Jake, can I come over?" Sharon said. This was the first time she had ever called me.

"Sure."

"Right now?"

"Uh, yeah, okay. I'll be out back."

She hung up. Her voice had sounded husky and low. She must have flown, because three minutes later she trotted around the back corner of my house onto the patio. I sat at a long picnic table. She dropped onto the bench across from me, breathing hard. At her feet she set a five-gallon paint bucket with a lid.

Her eyes stared into mine. She said nothing, but the sides of her nose flared out each time she breathed. The sun had recently set and the reddish light in the clouds made her eyes glow like an exotic jungle cat.

We stared at each other for a long time. She asked, "Do you have a shovel?"

"Yeah."

"Go get it."

She crackled with an energy that made me think asking questions right now was not a good idea. I hurried to the garage and fetched a garden spade. When I returned, she looked up at me.

"I want you to help me. I need to bury something."

"What is it?"

"Please, just dig a hole."

I led her to the eastern edge of the yard, under our peach trees, where the rich soil made it easy to dig. I scooped a hole out of the black dirt about two feet deep and a foot across. The damp soil smelled almost sweet. "Bigger?" I said.

"No, that's good."

She opened the paint bucket and reached inside. Her hands emerged holding a white bundle streaked with red.

"Pee-Wee?" I asked. Buzzing started in my head, like cicadas in August.

"He killed him."

"Who?"

"My bastard father."

"Why?"

The expression on her face shifted like mercury. First sad, then angry, then it went blank. She lowered the little dog into the hole. "Please, Jake, bury him."

I shoveled dirt onto the limp little form. Suddenly, a lump formed in my throat. Tears welled in my eyes. It was one thing when a turtle or a lizard died, but a dog? I knew this dog. I had played with him.

I gently patted down the final spadeful of dirt and crouched on the ground next to Sharon. She grasped my hand and her fire-eyes locked onto mine. "I came home and found him on the porch, crushed flat with blood all around his mouth. My father must have stomped him. The poor baby's ribs broke into smithereens."

The pressure on my hand increased until it hurt, but I didn't let go.

"I'm sorry, Sharon."

Her face contorted as she stared at the fresh dirt. I could barely hear her voice as she said, "I hate that man. He's determined to take away everything I love. First my sister, now my dog. Then, I guess, he'll kill me too."

A jolt ripped through me like the time I put my tongue on the terminals of a dry cell battery. A jolt of pure fear. I had suspected Sharon's father of her sister's death, but to hear it actually said was frightening, like in saying it, she made it real.

"Sharon, why do you think he killed Janey?"

Those eyes rolled wildly. "She was a thing to him. A creature he created to be whatever he wanted her to be."

"What do you mean?"

Her gaze swept toward the trees. "Jake, he started raping her when she was nine. She didn't know it was wrong. She thought she had to do whatever Daddy said. He trained her. All these years. A couple months ago, she told me. I have never felt so sad in my life. It took me weeks to convince her it was wrong. She was terrified. She had never stood up to him. But finally, she told him no."

Her eyes settled on mine. "She said no and the next day she was dead."

CHAPTER 32

It felt like an earthquake had ripped through my life, changing everything. I had never confronted evil, but here it grew, stark and horrible. I thought of the poor little girl her sister had been, crushed and humiliated for years, then thrown away like a doll.

Sharon's face held a fierce strength. It changed again. She became a child, bewildered and vulnerable.

"When you came over here last week... You said he tried it with you."

She nodded and tears suddenly poured down those soft cheeks. I had never done anything like this with a girl before, but I reached my arms around her and held her. She buried her face in my chest and made tiny sobbing sounds that broke my heart.

The sky darkened faster under the trees. I held her a long time. Her tears soaked the front of my shirt. When the mosquitoes became unbearable, we slowly got to our feet.

"Jake, can I stay here tonight?"

"Oh, God, Sharon, my parents."

"We can do like last time. I'll leave early. Please, I can't go home tonight."

"What about tomorrow night and the next?"

"I'll worry about that tomorrow."

"Okay."

How could I say no?

I went into my house and tried to act normal. Ten o'clock rolled around, then ten-thirty. Why were my parents still awake? Dad had to be up at the crack of dawn and on his construction site by seven. Mom left at seven-thirty for an office job. They normally turned in around ten. But here it was ten forty-five and they were still talking in the kitchen. Did they suspect something? God help me, what if Sharon showed up now?

Then it hit me. Today was Friday. No wonder they were in no hurry. No work tomorrow.

I drifted to the back porch and settled in a wicker chair. My mind went insane imagining Sharon strolling in wearing a see-through negligee, my parents swooping down on me, seeing her breasts, and chaining me in the basement, where I would just make more and more gunpowder until finally, driven out of my mind with captivity, I would set it off in the most god-awful blast ever seen in North America.

Even though the night felt cool, sweat poured off me like a glass of iced tea on a muggy day.

My parents finally went to bed around midnight.

Not wanting them to hear a peep out of me or even think of me at all, I waited until I heard their toilet flush to cover the sound of me opening the sofa bed on the porch. I waited. Around one, I heard scratching at the screen door. I let Sharon in and she glided through the shadows straight to my bed. She shucked her jeans and shoes and slipped under the covers. I sat next to her and stroked her head until I heard the rhythmic breathing of sleep.

I didn't even try to fall asleep. I didn't think I would ever sleep again as I gazed through the screens.

The lake was black. No moon yet. Fireflies streaked between the trees. Night air wafted through the windows, carrying the bright scent of the grass I had mowed that afternoon.

In that moment, I realized I was no longer a child. I no longer believed in innocence. My body would take years to catch up, but the damage was done. That's how I saw it. Damage. Once you sustained enough damage - once hard, ugly truths chipped away at you long enough - you became an adult.

I realized another ingredient of adulthood. Hate. I had never truly hated anything, but now hate lodged deep inside me like a hard nugget of pain. It changed me. I now understood why my father had never told me the most horrible things that happened in the war. Inside him lived the same hard hatred. He dared not let it out. He dared not let it pollute me or he would transform me from his child into a stranger, an adult who could hate just as hard as he could. We would become equals. And that was the job of parents, to keep that from happening as long as possible.

I have excellent hearing. My father sometimes would tease me by calling me bat-boy. I knew every sound that

150

was supposed to exist around my house, every scraping tree branch, every rustling shrub, every wave on the beach.

I now heard something that was not supposed to be there.

I heard breathing.

CHAPTER 33

I crept across the porch to the door. Usually, I left the solid door open and just the screen door closed, but now I gently pushed the heavy oak on its hinges. I turned the doorknob so that the door closed without a sound, then released the knob slowly. I quietly turned the deadbolt. To get in now, my visitor would have to jump twelve feet straight up just to reach the window screens. Getting through them would require the strength and gymnastic ability of an ape.

Crossing to the far end of the porch, I listened at a window, hearing the rustle of feet through grass, the quiet tread of someone stepping slowly across concrete. Too close. I waited until the footsteps were near the middle of the patio, my left hand on a light switch. I flicked it and the patio spotlights flared into life. Frozen for an instant, his eyes wide in shock, Ralph Young stared up at the windows. A heartbeat later, he vanished around the side of the house. I heard his boots hit the gravel at the edge of the street. They clomped on asphalt and rapidly diminished in the distance.

Backwash from the spotlights lit up the porch. Sharon stirred. I flipped off the lights.

When I sat on the bed, she said, "What happened?"

"Your brother paid us a visit."

"He follows me sometimes. He's like a ghost. I never know when he'll appear."

"Do you think he followed you or did he just suspect you might be here?"

"He must have followed me."

"He's gone now."

She settled into the bed. I got under the covers. She reached for my hand.

I laid there a long time thinking about how I no longer felt safe in my own home.

CHAPTER 34
July 26, 1965

Sharon left before dawn. This time I heard her go, but I rolled over and slept a couple more hours. I threw on a bathing suit and a blue Yankees T-shirt and stumbled into the kitchen. My dad's car keys lay in the center of the table. Where Paul usually sat was a half-eaten Pop-Tart, a puddle of milk, and a universe of crumbs. The demon spawn was up.

The stove clock said 8:05. I didn't hear anyone moving around. Tiptoeing into the hall, I found the door to my parents' bedroom closed. That meant it was locked too. God help us if we disturbed them on a weekend.

More better. I didn't want to explain my next moves to anybody. I crept down the stairs and used the basement phone to call Munson's office, expecting to leave a message, but he was there.

"You work on Saturday?" I said.

Munson barked, "I work every goddamn day of the week, twenty-four hours a day when bodies pop up faster than dandelions in my lawn. You have another one?"

"Sounds like you need some sleep, Lieutenant."

"I'll sleep when I'm dead. What's on your mind?"

"Something happened. Something I need to tell you."

"Shoot."

"No, I'm home. If my parents hear me... I don't want them to know this."

"Okay, I'll be over in thirty minutes. We can talk outside."

"Not at my house."

"Why not?"

"I don't need the attention. Can you meet me at the public beach across the lake in half an hour?" He agreed.

I debated whether to go upstairs and have breakfast. If my parents woke up, I'd have to answer questions. Maybe just better to git while the gittin's good.

I sauntered down the lawn behind my house. Ten minutes of rowing and I'd be across the lake, leaving time to collect my thoughts before Munson arrived. At least, that was the plan. As I rounded the peach trees I froze.

Our dock was empty. No boat. So much for plans.

Running the rest of the way to the shore, I spied my brother parked in a patch of lily pads about fifty feet off the western border of our yard. Paul knelt motionless in the boat near shore, his long-handled net poised above the water.

"Hey, snotbag," I shouted as I approached.

"Ssshhhh," he hissed without turning his head.

I scanned the lily pads. A small painted turtle lazed in the center of one of the broader leaves. Paul's net inched toward the green and red reptile.

"I need my boat."

"It's not *your* boat." He didn't even move his lips, like he was a master puppeteer.

"I don't have time for your crap, you little weasel. Get over here."

"After I catch this turtle."

"No. Now."

"Bite me."

"Paul, I need to get across the lake. Now."

"Gotta meet the girlfriend? The one who buys all her clothes four sizes too small?"

"I said NOW!"

"Swim across. I'm busy." His net crept another inch closer to the unsuspecting turtle. I have to admit, my brother had great turtle-catching skills. He had infinite patience.

I was amazed I'd let the conversation get this far. Talk was worthless with Paul. I grabbed a chunk of sandstone off the beach and hucked it at the base of the boat. The stone splashed inches from the turtle. The little creature rocketed across its lily pad a fraction of an inch ahead of Paul's net, then dove and disappeared. "Okay, Paul, you're not busy now."

Paul's face turned red as he glared at me. "I'll kill you." His shout bounced around the cove.

"Come over and do it."

He was not far from shore, so I decided to surprise him. Sprinting across the narrow strand, I dove into the green water. Lily pad stalks grabbed at me like a net. If the water had been clear, I would have surfaced next to the boat, but impeded by the vegetation, I came up five feet short.

The oars splashed and the light vessel pulled away quickly. I swam as fast as I could, but within seconds, Paul pulled out of reach.

"Paul, goddammit."

"I can't heearrrrr you. Louder please. Let Mom hear you cursing."

"You don't give me that boat, you better stay out there forever."

He circled me, twenty feet away, making faces and farting noises.

"I need the boat, goddammit. I need to get across the lake."

"Aren't you like some kind of champion swimmer?" He pulled away. I would never catch him.

"Crap." I began an energy-conserving breast stroke. I had swum the lake a million times. I just needed to do it again.

Twenty minutes later, as I hauled myself onto the public beach, Munson strolled down the grassy hill. So much for collecting my thoughts. He crossed fifty feet of sand and didn't even comment that I had just climbed out of the lake panting. "Damn, I got sand in my shoes now," he grumbled, leaning over to empty his left shoe.

"Lieutenant, you're at a beach. What do you expect?"

He made a fuss about emptying the other shoe, a black loafer with tassels. I never understood why a man's shoes needed tassels. I didn't see anything fall out of it, but maybe Munson had sensitive skin and could actually feel one grain of sand.

"What's the plan, Jake? We stand out here in the sun so I can bake in my suit?"

"No, follow me."

I led him along a path into a wooded area. A fallen oak provided a good place to sit.

"Why all the cloak and dagger?"

"Lieutenant, I'm going to tell you something. Don't interrupt with questions 'cause I want to get this out of me all at once. Okay?"

He nodded. I told him what Sharon Young had told me the previous night. True to his word, he didn't

157

interrupt. When I finished, he stared across the water. After a minute, he said, "Did she see her father kill her sister?"

'No."

"Did she see him rape her sister?"

"No."

"Is there a weapon or something he used to kill Janey?"

"No."

"So, it's just her suspicion. There's no evidence."

I thought my head would explode. "You're kidding me."

"No, I'm being a cop. What her sister told her can't be proven. It's hearsay. Her sister isn't around to corroborate it. What Sharon Young suspects her father of doing is speculation. She didn't see a crime, she didn't see him dump a body. There's no murder weapon. There's nothing the District Attorney could take into court."

"You're not serious."

"Jake, I'm willing to agree that the father might have killed Janey Young. I'm willing to believe everything her sister told you. The only problem is that none of it's provable. There's no case. I can't arrest people without evidence."

"Crap."

"Yeah, I agree."

We stayed silent a long while. Munson broke the stillness. "Get anything about Janey's pregnancy?"

I froze, but I tried to look like I was thinking. From what Chaz had said a couple nights ago, he had screwed Janey Young. He could have gotten her pregnant. Was he really the father? Would he kill her to hide that fact? If I told Munson what he said, Munson would turn Chaz's life upside down. I couldn't believe Chaz was capable of murder, but his switchblade was missing. Had he cut out Janey Young's eyes?

I hate my mind. It goes crazy sometimes. In circles. If Chaz killed Janey, why would he admit to me he'd screwed her? Because he didn't know she was pregnant? If he didn't know, there was no reason to kill her. Yet if he did, wouldn't he want to hide the fact he was involved with her and not tell me about banging her?

Why was I going over this? Chaz didn't matter. From what Sharon told me last night, I had no doubt that old man Young was the culprit.

"You still with me, Jake?"

"Yeah, sorry, I was up late last night." I knew the danger of lying to Munson. Either way I took this, I'd feel like I made a mistake. I said, "No, I can't really ask about her being pregnant without showing that I know about it. And how would I know? So, I just talk about Janey and hope somebody will blab that she was pregnant. So far, no blabbing."

"I wonder if she had a pregnancy test. I have people checking into that."

"That's it?"

"No, we're looking at other stuff, but if she had a pregnancy test, there might be something in the medical record. Maybe we get lucky and her father took her to the doctor. I need something to show motive. If he knew she was pregnant, that could be enough to dig deeper."

"Lieutenant, how do you handle the stuff we talk about?"

"What do you mean?"

"Like in your reports. Do you mention me?"

"No, I just use what you tell me to look into things, maybe change direction. Why?"

"Rubino. Why does he have such a hair up his ass about me? He said I'm trying to ruin an innocent man's life. How would he know what I'm saying? Or that I'm saying anything at all?"

"Jake, I swear, I've protected you. No way I'd let a kid get famous from a thing like this."

"You don't put me in your reports, but do you talk to other detectives about me?"

"No, I mean it, no. What we talk about is just between us."

"Have you checked out Rubino?"

"Yeah. As much as I can without rousing suspicions."

"And?"

"He was on duty the night she died."

"He has a squad car, right?"

"Yeah."

"He's alone, right?"

159

"I know where you're going."

I pushed on anyway. "Lieutenant, just because he was on duty doesn't mean he wasn't with Janey. Have you checked the car he was in?"

"Yeah. Last week. After he went off shift, I had a lab guy go over it. There was no blood in it, no long black hair in the trunk."

"Can you trust the lab guy? What if he tells Rubino? One more reason for Rubino to get me."

"The lab guy's my cousin. Relax."

My eyes dropped to my feet. I toed a rock out of the sand.

"Feelin' down, Jake?"

"Yeah. I thought what Sharon told me would be the end of it. Buddy Young in the electric chair."

"It's not how the system works."

"Yeah, well don't expect me to come see you after graduation. I don't think I'll be a cop."

"Would you rather get up a posse and go lynch him?"

"That's a plan."

"You can't take the law into your own hands, Jake."

"Then what good is the law?"

CHAPTER 35

I swam back across the lake. Munson had offered me a ride, but I told him I needed to cool off or he'd have to arrest me later in the day.

"What for?" he said.

"My brother. He might have a serious accident."

The swim gave me a chance to think. Was Munson telling the truth? He seemed like a straight shooter. He didn't like Rubino, that was clear. He had no reason to tell Rubino anything. So, what made Rubino and Buddy Young so insane about me? Maybe Munson had made an offhand remark to someone at the police station and had forgotten about it. Somehow, what I said had gotten to Rubino.

I slogged up the hill. I entered the basement door, toweled off, and threw on a dry T-shirt. I heard voices upstairs. Oh, no, everyone was up. Full house. Mom, Dad, little twerp brother.

The smell of pancakes filled the kitchen. Sausages sizzled in a frying pan. My mother happily performed her ritual of taking care of her family on the two days she could.

As I entered the kitchen, my mom said, "How many pancakes, Jake?" She seemed absolutely bubbly. At times like this, wearing green pedal-pushers and a T-shirt, with her auburn hair pulled back in a ponytail, and her green eyes flashing, she looked like she wasn't much older than me.

I glared at Paul. He leaned his head back and forth as if he heard music and half-closed his eyes as he stuffed a gigantic chunk of pancake into his mouth. He chewed, opening his mouth wide so I could see. He wanted me to lose control in front of Mom and Dad so he could be the victim. I wasn't playing that game. He'd pay later.

"No thanks, Mom. Not hungry," I said.

My dad jumped on that. "Whoa, Charlie Brown, you don't want pancakes? You sick?"

"Do I have to be eating all the time to be well?"

My parents exchanged a glance. My mother said, "Jake, who was that girl last night?"

Oh, my God, they knew. My mouth turned to sand as Paul eyeballed me. Had he been creeping around last night? That little ferret, squealer, sneak. How would I explain Sharon in my bed?

"Ugh, well..."

"The one who called, the one in the back yard, who is she?"

I saw some daylight. Maybe this was just curiosity about the phone call. "She's a friend."

"A bit old for you, Jake. She's a woman."

Dad said, "Was she the one in the bikini?"

Oh, great.

"What bikini?" Mom said.

Paul chirped in right on cue with his sing-song twerpy little brother act. "Jake has a girlfriend. A half-naked girlfriend." He chanted and sashayed around his chair, wiggling his hips and kissing the air. I wanted to set him on fire.

Mom surprised me. She pointed at Paul. "Out! Take your food and go on the porch."

"But, Mom..."

"I said out. And take a napkin."

"Yeah, slob-o-miser." I couldn't resist adding my two cents.

"Yeah, smooch-o-miser," he crooned as he rolled his hips all the way out of the kitchen.

"Sma-a-a-l-l-l Paul."

"Have a nice swim?" he tossed over his shoulder.

"Mom, next time I have to baby sit, I'm putting him on an inner tube and pushing him to the middle of the lake. Like Moses. Some other family can find him. Just so you know."

"You'll do no such thing. Now, what did you two bury under the peach trees?"

Okay, so that's what this was about. The overnight aspect of Sharon's visit was still unknown. I saw no point dragging things out. "Her dog."

My mother spun around from the stove. "What?"

"Her dog died and she wanted to bury it here."

"Why here?"

"In view of the lake. It was important to her. Should I have said no?"

"No. I was just curious. So, who is she?"

I debated this one. I opted for truth. "Sharon Young."

My mother's eyebrows lifted and wrinkles carved into her forehead. "Is she the sister of the girl that..that...well, that you found?"

"Yeah."

"Oh, poor baby. She lost her sister and then her dog? I understand."

I didn't know what she understood, but she stopped asking questions.

My secret non-sex-life was safe. So far.

CHAPTER 36

Problems. As evening approached, my parents fussed around like they had plans to go out. If I got roped into watching Paul I had no doubt that today would be the day I'd kill him and I'd go to jail and probably have the bad luck of having Buddy Young as my cellmate.

However, if I left the premises, I might run into, let's see: Rubino. He'd arrest me. Unless he was the killer. Then he'd weigh me down with cinder blocks and dump me in the lake. His daughter, Angie; she'd try to scratch my eyes out. Ralph; he'd stomp me into a greasy stain on the street. Ralph's father; he'd probably burn me with the trash and I'd disappear like the wagon. Hmm, yes, Carl Hardwick and Animal would surely have plans for me; that would be the choking death. Who else had I pissed off? There had to be someone else out there. I was sure that psychopaths I had never met wandered the streets hoping to find me. In the space of a few weeks I had gone from anonymous to Most-Likely-To-Be-Murdered.

I suppose I'm an optimist, because I hopped on my bike and decided to visit Eddie. Maybe he'd want to fly his gas-engine planes before it got dark. Maybe, if I was lucky, I'd catch a glimpse of Sharon as I passed her house. Halfway up the hill to Eddie's a siren blipped behind me. My second worst nightmare, Rubino.

I couldn't believe it, but the loudspeaker came on. "Pull over."

Pull over? I was doing four in a thirty mile an hour zone. On a *bicycle.* Pull over? I'd never heard such total crap.

I stopped at the side of the street and Rubino drove up next to me. He didn't get out of the car, just sat there scowling at me through the open passenger window. The police car engine whirred and the hot metal ticked. "My daughter has two black eyes."

"Yeah, now they match yours, except hers are temporary." I stared at him. No way I was apologizing.

If he had rabies, he couldn't look more crazed. The car was his cage and he knew it. He couldn't get at me from the driver's seat. "You're in a lot of trouble, kid."

"Why?"

"Troublemakers always get in trouble."

"Oh, wow, that's really deep. Insightful. Compelling."

Rubino squinted at me as if I'd spoken Greek. Okay, showing off my vocabulary wasn't the best move at this point. "Get in the car," he said. "I wanna talk to you."

"I can hear you just fine from right here." I hunched down over my bike to talk through the passenger window. "So talk."

His lips pressed together. I weighed my options. He weighed his. To grab me, he had to get out of the car. That gave me maybe five seconds to get my bike up to speed and get away. No sweat. I was on a hill and would accelerate fast. By the time he got back in his car, I'd pull a Houdini. Yeah, I was fine if I didn't get into the car. He couldn't do anything about it.

"You got some personal reason to cause Buddy Young so much trouble?"

Three weeks ago, I would have withered, but I had the devil in me now. I wasn't the same person. "Maybe you should ask him why he beats his kids so much. How about incest, Officer Rubino? You think you could keep your friend away from his own daughters?"

"You're nuts, kid."

"Or maybe you think it's okay. Maybe that's why your own daughter's so screwed up."

See? My big mouth. Why couldn't I leave Angie out of this? Rubino's face transformed from day to night like a super-fast eclipse. I thought he looked pissed when he pulled up on me, but now? God, I thought every blood vessel in his forehead would burst.

I didn't wait to see what would happen. I knew what would happen.

I wheeled around and pedaled downhill. Started right in third gear. Hauled ass. I heard gravel flying all over as Rubino slewed his cruiser around. I had about seven seconds before that big V-8 Plymouth chewed right up my tail. I had to make the side street.

No Tour de France bikers ever pedaled the way I did. Those guys raced to win a trophy. I raced to save my life. I didn't need Dad's advice on how to go fast. No big Mako could possibly scare me more than having a crazed Rubino behind me.

My fifty foot lead on the Plymouth wouldn't last long. No way for a bike to outrun a car, but the advantage of the bike was the ability to change direction and go places a car couldn't.

Flipping left around a corner I heard Rubino's tires grind into the turn. I cut down a driveway, knowing this house didn't have a fence between its back yard and the next house. My bike vibrated across gravel, then lawn, then down the concrete driveway of the next house onto another street.

I tore right on Lincoln Avenue, a dead-end street that ended at the woods. If I could get there, Rubino could not follow. The woods was my best bet. My home right now would be radioactive.

Sweat poured into my eyes, heat sweat and fear sweat, burning my eyelids like acid. With the temperature in the nineties and the sun chewing into my back, my legs churned like an egg beater.

Tires screeched half a block back as Rubino rounded the corner to get on my street. I chanced a quick glance over my shoulder. I had maybe a hundred-yard lead. I had to go another hundred yards. My speedometer said thirty-five. Rubino would have to do over seventy to get to the end of the street before I did.

I heard that monster cop engine torque up, heard the tires bite into the asphalt. Forget seventy. That car could do 120.

My leg muscles burned like molten metal ran through the veins. My heart sounded like the bass drum in a rock group. The muscles in my jaw ached from clamping my teeth down so hard. Something was going to break or burst or get real messy if I didn't stop. Then dancing lights appeared on the edges of my vision. No, no, fainting would be fatal. Damn my screwed up heart valve. Primal fear kept me going. I needed just a few more seconds. A big shark wanted me. I had to hang on.

I hit forty as the V-8 growled closer. I even heard the wind whistling across the surface of Rubino's cruiser. He was that close. I didn't dare look back now. At this speed, the slightest mistake equaled disaster.

Ahead, a galvanized barrier marked the end of the street. A yellow reflective sign sat on the middle of the barrier. Four wooden posts in the ground supported the barrier where the asphalt ended. On either side was a narrow opening where people passed to get to the trail leading into the woods. The left opening was lined up directly with the trail. I aimed for it.

I had fifty feet to go. It felt like I pedaled through molasses. I moved so slowly and the car moved so fast. Any second I expected its bumper to crush my spine.

Just twenty more feet. Yet it seemed to take longer than the entire distance I had already covered.

The V-8 roared in my ears. I started to feel dizzy. My teeth ached. I only needed a few more seconds.

I concentrated on the narrow gap between the end of the metal barrier and the maple that grew next to it. Two feet of opening. I'd made it through a million times, but at much slower speeds.

A screech tore the air behind me, Rubino hitting the brakes. It sounded like some prehistoric beast wailing in agony. The barrier loomed up too quickly. If either side of my handlebars hit anything, I'd be flipped into a pretzel. Maimed. Crippled. I focused. Stopped pedaling. Stopped breathing. Sat perfectly still. Aimed.

I shot through the gap and launched into the air, like trying to make a perfect high-dive. You start in brightness and heat and you fall through space all tensed and straight until you hit the water and relax in the coolness. Once you're airborne, there's nothing else you can do. Either your set-up is correct, or you wind up in the hospital. I crossed the line of demarcation between sun and shade in mid-air. But now in the deep shadows of massive oaks and maples, I was blind. I hung onto my bike. Stayed motionless. Panic was not the solution. If I stayed still, the trail would rise to meet me. I just had to be ready and keep my feet on the pedals so I wouldn't twist off the bike.

The trail was below street level. I must have flown thirty feet before my wheels touched down. The seat rammed into me like I'd been kicked in the groin, but I whooped with joy. I had just set a new airborne record, though with no witnesses. I concentrated on hitting my brakes gently enough that I didn't spin out as I kicked up an enormous cloud of dust from the dirt path.

Behind me it sounded like a bulldozer scraping its blade on the street. That would be Rubino skidding on the gravel in the dead-end. I heard a loud thump, then massive hissing.

I had to look, I just had to, even at the risk of losing control and smashing into a tree. A plume of steam rose from the front of Rubino's cruiser which was mashed against the dead-end barrier. A string of curses hailed me until I pulled out of earshot.

I smiled. The end of the street had lots of loose gravel because nobody drove on a dead-end. Only a kid who spent his life being chased would know that. Rubino didn't have the encyclopedic knowledge of every street in the neighborhood that I had.

Too bad. Let him explain that to his sergeant.

CHAPTER 37

Now I had a bigger problem. I couldn't go home. I couldn't go to any of my friends' houses because if the cops came after me, those were the first places they'd look. My immediate future depended on what Rubino did. A normal human being might realize that losing control and trying to run down a kid was not something you'd want to make public, but Rubino wasn't normal. Yeah, he'd come up with Plan B. He'd lie. He'd pin the blame on me. He was that kind of prick.

Which meant I could go nowhere familiar.

As I pushed through the woods, a musty smell of decaying leaves wafted up from the earth. The trail petered out. I tucked my bike into a thicket and hiked to the sandstone cliffs, sat with my feet hanging over the edge as the sun melted toward the horizon. The cliffs below glowed in the hellish light. Heat rose off the sandstone and brought to my nose the sharp dryness of rock along with the sweet dampness of algae. The surface of the lake transformed to molten bronze.

Below was my formerly favorite thinking place. I focused on the tree stretching out over the pike pool, the place I had found Janey Young's hair. I glanced on either side of me. Within a few feet of this spot, Janey Young had been thrown away like a piece of trash.

Or did she jump? I couldn't buy that one. Why would a pretty girl want to leave a mangled corpse?

The liquid metal under the tree roiled and a fish broke the surface. Some drama unfolded down there. Big fish, little fish. Somebody was dinner.

I never wanted to fish from that tree again. Even sitting here on the cliff made me nervous, but I wanted to visualize what Munson had warned me about. I estimated where on the lake I was that evening when I thought I heard a scream. From up here, it would have been impossible not to have seen my aluminum boat.

Looking down, why would I think of high school physics? Why would my crazy little brain calculate the distance down and the acceleration of a falling body? I didn't want to know how Janey Young's head smashed into the tree trunk. My nights were already plagued by heart-stopping nightmares of a switchblade mangling her eye sockets. I didn't need more horrific images in my head. The answer came anyway. She hit the tree about fifty-five miles per hour. That's like jumping out of a car on the turnpike.

The sun would soon be gone. What would I do? I had nowhere to go, no money. It wasn't like in the movies where I could hop a freight train and start life in a new city. I was too young. Eventually, I'd have to go home and the hammer would fall on me.

I had gotten in way over my head. Because of a crush on Sharon Young? Because I wanted to help Munson? Or because I thought I was so damn smart?

So, now my face had splashed across the front page with a headline that I was helping the police. I had found no proof against Buddy Young or anybody else, but that damn reporter made it sound like I knew something. He stirred up enough of a mess that the killer had to see me as a threat. The killer could see me, but I was blind to him. A perfect target. A perfect stupid little target.

A branch cracked somewhere back in the woods. Bat-boy hearing told me that feet shuffled over leaves. So my killer was clumsy. Or he didn't care. Why should he? I was trapped on a finger of sandstone and had nowhere to go except back into the woods toward him or over the edge to my death. In a few seconds, he could just run up and push me off the cliff, like Janey. The circle would be complete. Another body in the lake.

More footsteps. I had a crazy idea that if I didn't do anything nothing would happen. A second would go by, then another. I could stay just like this, forever frozen in time like a fossilized ant in amber.

If I turned around, everything would change. But how could I not look? Who would it be? Rubino. Or Ralph. Or Buddy Young. Who would be my executioner? Yet I had to know. I had to turn. If someone had come to kill me, I deserved to know who. In slow-motion, I rotated my head.

He stepped off the path and came out from under the trees.

CHAPTER 38

He marched straight to the cliff and sat five feet to my right, hanging his skinny legs over the edge. I couldn't believe it. Georgie. Goddamn little maniac Georgie Blanco.

I wanted to scream in relief that it wasn't Rubino. But I just said, "Hey, Georgie."

He stared right at me. He seldom made eye contact with anybody, but this time Georgie's furtive blue eyes settled on my face for several seconds. He still had scabs on his cheeks from the beating Ralph had given him. The black-eye bruising had faded to something approximating women's eye shadow.

In the late sun his hair gleamed like metal. His hair didn't lay down like normal hair. Each strand of his crew-cut stuck straight out. He looked like a bronze porcupine.

"Whatcha doin', Georgie?"

He stared at the water far below.

"You ever been here before?"

"Yeah," he said.

My heart was still pounding from my Rubino escape, so I stared at the far shore and took a few deep breaths. Pushing Georgie to do anything was impossible. It would be like trying to pick up mercury between two fingers.

"You found her, right?" he said.

"Uh-huh."

I had never had a conversation with Georgie. I didn't know he could concentrate long enough to have a conversation.

"I heard her scream," he said.

Far off a duck squawked. An electric blue dragonfly hovered around the toe of my sneaker. A bee buzzed past my ear with the sound I imagined a bullet would make if it just missed my head. My heart speeded up again. I would need more air.

Georgie was a fish nibbling at bait. If I jerked the hook, he'd take off. I had to be patient, wait for him to swallow that hook, make sure he didn't get away before I heard the rest.

"Janey? You heard her scream?" I said, just to be sure.

He nodded.

"Where were you?"

This question scared me with sudden visions of Georgie throwing Janey Young off the cliff. I leaned back from the edge and pulled my feet under me, ready to spring up if I needed to. I had a sudden fear he might throw *me* off the cliff. I didn't want to make it too easy.

He pointed down at the shore, halfway around the small cove. Okay, he hadn't been up here. That was a good thing.

"What were you doing?"

"Catchin' frogs."

He didn't look like he would run off. He seemed calmer than I had ever seen him. Georgie Blanco on simmer for a change.

"What did you see, Georgie?"

"The splash. I looked up. I saw the splash."

"And you heard a scream?"

"Yeah."

"A girl's scream?"

"Yeah."

Would Janey scream as she committed suicide? Maybe if she changed her mind halfway down. Georgie had just jumbled the pieces of the puzzle into a new shape.

"Did you tell anyone?"

"No."

"Why not?"

One corner of his mouth went up, the other went down. "They'd think I did it."

"But it was Janey? You're sure?"

"Had to be. Next day you found her body."

My heart hammered. I was very close to fainting. I remembered the evening Georgie described, the one I had told Munson about. Whoever was up here would have seen me on the water. My shiny aluminum boat was hard to miss. I had the only one like it on the lake. If Janey Young had been murdered, her killer knew I was a possible witness within seconds of committing the crime. It felt real now. The danger I was in.

Now for the big one. I had to set this hook. "Georgie, did you see anyone up here on the cliff?" Please, Georgie, please. I prayed for the answer.

He shook his head. "No."

"You're sure?"

"I heard the scream. I saw the splash. When I looked up here, I didn't see nothin'."

Great. Did she kill herself or did someone do it for her? I still didn't know.

"What did you do then?"

"I ran."

He ran? Why should I believe his story? In the entire universe of random occurrences, what were the chances that Georgie would be in the exact spot that a murder took place? Maybe this little lunatic hadn't been catching frogs at all. Maybe he didn't see anyone up here because *he* was up here. And why was he here now? Revisiting the scene of his crime? I pushed further back from the cliff edge, just in case.

He looked at me again. "So, what are *you* doin' here?"

I had to tell him something to keep him quiet about seeing me. He hated Rubino, so maybe the simple truth was my best bet. "Hiding. Rubino's after me."

"Yeah?" His eyes lit up.

I told him the story.

"He crashed the copmobile?" It was like he'd just blown out the candles on his birthday cake and immediately got his wish.

I couldn't help but smile. "Yeah."

The image of it was too much for Georgie. He rose off simmer and heated up right before my eyes, heading for boil. Mind dancing, eyeballs twitching. I tried to change his direction.

"Can you keep a secret?" I said.

"No."

Just like that. Maybe telling him the truth hadn't been the best bet.

"George, if you tell anybody where I am, Rubino will find out. He'll kill me if he finds me. He'll throw me right off this cliff and walk away and he'll tell people I committed suicide."

It was the wrong thing to say. Georgie went to full boil, his normal, agitated state. He'd probably hustle over to Rubino's house and tell him I was here, just so he

175

could watch Rubino throw me off the cliff. It didn't matter that he hated Rubino. A good show was a good show.

Georgie had no allegiance to me or anybody. He was like a cherry bomb after the fuse was lit. I remembered the standard instructions on fireworks packages: Light fuse, retire quickly.

"Well, I'm goin' home. The only person who can help me is my father," I announced.

Having foolishly ignited Georgie's fuse, I hustled into the trees in the direction of home. As soon as I was deep in the shadows, I cut north, away from my house. Home was the last place I could go. I jogged up a narrow game trail to get as far from Georgie as possible. I figured I had maybe twenty minutes before the little maggot's mouth exploded to somebody.

I had to know what Rubino was doing and I had to find out fast.

I traversed the woods and slunk through some back yards to the corner store. It had a pay phone. I found some change in my pocket and a crumpled up dollar.

"Munson."

"Lieutenant, it's Jake."

"Must be important for you to interrupt your busy day."

"It is." I wrestled with telling him what Georgie had told me, but Georgie's story raised more questions than it answered. I needed Munson's help with a much bigger problem. Right now. I couldn't have him running off after Georgie and leaving me to Rubino's tender mercies. So, I told him what happened with Rubino.

"Jake, that was about the stupidest thing you could have done."

"I know. But I didn't really *do* anything. Rubino just overreacted."

"Overreacted?" Munson laughed. "Yeah, Tony always overreacts when people accuse him of molesting his daughter. I can't understand it. Such an overly sensitive guy."

"Okay, okay, you got me. I have a big stupid mouth. So, what do I do?"

"Y'know, Jake, I'm supposed to go off duty in fifteen minutes. My wife will have dinner waiting for me. She's a good cook. I don't often get to have dinner with my wife."

"At least you can go home, Lieutenant. I can't. I'll have to sleep outside, under a bush or behind somebody's garage. The mosquitoes will feast on me all night and tomorrow I'll look like the Elephant Man."

He sighed. "Look, keep out of sight. Let me see what Rubino's stirring up at this end. Can you call me around nine?"

"Okay." I hung up.

I surveyed the street before stepping into the corner store. I had enough money for Big Bob to slice some ham and make me a sandwich. I bought an orange juice and kept two dimes for phone calls. One for Munson. One for my mother. Better get that one over with.

"Mom, I'm at Eddie's. We had dinner."

"I wish you'd let me know ahead of time. I had fried chicken ready for you."

"Sorry, Mom."

"Coming home soon? It's almost eight."

"Can I stay at Eddie's? There's a monster movie on TV."

"Okay. Just call me later."

I got away from the store and its traffic and the eyes that might see me. Then it hit me.

The safest place in a hurricane is the eye of the storm.

CHAPTER 39

I avoided cars. As soon as I saw one, I slipped behind a bush or hedge. Approaching Sharon's house, I slipped under the sprawling umbrella of a forsythia bush at the corner of the yard. I could wait undetected and go back to the pay phone and call Munson later. Nobody would imagine I'd hide in Buddy Young's yard.

I had trouble moving my legs. I had trouble moving anything once I relaxed. Right after the bike chase, I had enough adrenaline to leap a tall building. My encounter with Georgie tuned me up again. Now, after eating the sandwich, I couldn't keep my eyes open.

It's strange that in the middle of the biggest crisis of my life, I fell asleep. Just curled up, put my head on my forearm, and drifted off. My dad had told me he had done the same thing in the war. Whenever he had a chance to sleep, he slept, whatever mayhem might be happening.

When I awoke, I couldn't see anything in the pitch black under the bush. How long had I slept? I panicked. I didn't have a wristwatch, but to be this dark it was way past nine. What had Munson thought when I missed my deadline to call? Was he now looking for me too? If I called the station, would he still be there, waiting, missing dinner with his wife?

I heard voices raised in the Young house, not loud enough to carry far, but with ugly undertones. The sharp gutturals of Buddy Young and the piping voice of Ralph built in intensity.

The voices stopped. I heard crashing, thumps. I slunk closer to the house, hearing impacts, grunts.

Shadows passed over the curtains on the first floor. A fight.

The old frame house shook. I was crazy scared, but I crept up to a living room window where light beamed out. Standing next to the foundation, I slowly rose until my eyes came just even with the sill. For a second I saw an empty room, then Ralph slid across the floor. A step behind him Buddy Young loomed like a grizzly. His big paws reached out, grabbed Ralph by an arm, and hauled him to his feet. One of the paws curled into a fist. I watched in fascination as the fist drew back slowly. As if released on a spring, it snapped into Ralph's stomach.

Through the open window, I heard a loud grunt as the air exploded from Ralph's lungs. The fist retracted and, like a piston, slammed into Ralph's face again and again with exactly the same motion and force each time. That fist moved like a machine designed to inflict pain in exact increments. If I had been hit like that, I would have screamed like a banshee, but Ralph just grunted. He must have learned to take a beating silently so the neighbors wouldn't get nosy.

Blood poured out of Ralph's mouth. The fist came down like a hammer on his temple and Ralph stopped moving. Like a cat discarding a mouse after the fun had gone out of it, Young turned away from his son's crumpled body. He glared around the living room as if getting his bearings and finally settled in a stuffed chair. He wiped blood from his fist onto the leg of his jeans. Then he grabbed a brown bottle off the end table and lifted it to his lips. I watched his Adam's apple bounce up and down a few times. Then his head drooped.

I wished I was older. I wanted to go in there and thrash that bastard.

I didn't like Ralph, but this wasn't a fair fight. It made me sick to see Ralph clubbed senseless by fists like sledgehammers.

How could a father bring children into the world and use them like things? When I thought of my own disputes with my parents, they paled in comparison. Having my allowance reduced if I didn't mow the lawn by Saturday afternoon seemed a ridiculous penance. These kids had never heard of allowance, except maybe their weekly beatings.

Ralph's head lolled to one side and he swallowed. Well, he hadn't died. Yet.

Where was Sharon? For a moment I had forgotten about her. I envisioned her upstairs in a pool of blood.

Hunkering under the window, I trotted around the side of the house to the rose trellis. Nobody had trimmed these roses for years and they grew so thick, I could barely squeeze my feet onto the rungs. Thorns tore at my bare skin, but I continued struggling up until I came to the second floor balcony that wrapped around the back of the house. I stepped over the rickety railing and crept past the window I knew to be Ralph's room, around the corner, to the doorway that serviced the balcony. It was locked. I continued along the wall to Sharon's bedroom. A low glow came from the window. I was afraid to look inside.

When I peeked around the window frame, I stopped breathing. Sharon's body stretched across the bed like a rag doll, face-down, naked and unmoving. A sheet partially covered her. Abandoning caution, I clawed at the half-open window sash, hauled it up. As I stepped over the window sill, Sharon's head turned and her eyes jerked around in their sockets. For a second she didn't recognize me.

"Sharon, it's me." I hurried to the side of her bed and knelt down, so our eyes were level. That's when I saw the clothesline that tied her wrists and ankles to the bed frame.

For a second, her fear dissolved and she looked at me with recognition. Then her body shook. She said, "Get out of here, Jake. Hurry. Please."

"No. You're coming with me." I clawed at one of the cords.

"Where can I go?" Her voice was hopeless.

"To my house for now. Call the police."

She shook her head. "You don't understand. He'll find me."

"Not if he's in jail."

The door burst open and Buddy Young hulked into the room. "Ain't nobody goin' to jail."

I stepped back as the air itself pushed against me. Up close, Young felt like a force of nature. Like he had his own electric field. Those big sausage-fingered hands scared the hell out of me as I imagined them closing around my neck like the coils of a python.

"We take care of our own business in this family."

I edged back until my thighs rested against the window sill. My heart spasmed like it wanted to crawl out of my chest.

I couldn't fight with this man. He dwarfed me. He had thrown Ralph around like a toy and Ralph was one of the toughest guys in the neighborhood. Buddy now stood between Sharon and me. I had no way to get her out of this room, away from this house.

"Yeah, well, this time your family business ends, you sack of shit. The police know you killed your daughter." I spat it out, not caring what I said.

"That's what you been tellin' 'em? Nosin' around here, *Little Sherlock*? You lyin' little rat bastard."

The odor of alcohol hit me.

Young stepped toward me and the hate in his eyes sent me into panic mode. I had no doubt those sausage fingers would squeeze the life out of me. I hated myself as I spun and dove through the open window. I hit the porch and scraped my hands and knees, but I didn't feel pain. Fear and disgust eclipsed everything; fear of what those sausage hands would do to me, disgust that my fear had pushed me to abandon Sharon.

I ran around the corner to the rose trellis. The heavy clump of work boots vibrated the porch behind me. I turned in time to see Buddy Young lunging for me. No time for climbing down the trellis. I threw my legs over the railing, pushed off with my hands, and jumped into the darkness. I couldn't see the ground, couldn't gauge the distance. I hit the grass and rolled as I had seen paratroopers do in the movies. A lightning bolt of pain shot up through my feet and ripped into my guts. My diaphragm locked up the way it had when Ralph punched me a million years ago. I laid on the damp grass, stunned.

I tried to stand. Nothing wanted to work. I needed air. I heard a screen door slam and I knew my life could be measured in mere moments.

How long did I have? I couldn't wait for the timer to release my diaphragm. My life focused to just one second at a time. Push off the ground with your hands. Get your legs under you. Take a step. Ignore the pain.

"Hey, you little bastard sonofabitch!"

Ignore the stars at the edge of your vision. Move the other leg. Try to take a breath.

"I'm gonna twist yer head off like a chicken."

Now run!

What I did next couldn't be called running, but at least I was moving. I hobbled toward the hedge, toward the break I knew to be there. I forced a small breath into my throat. With each step, my body responded slightly better. A fast walk, then a slow run. Through the hedge into the darkness under the neighbor's trees. Now a trot as my lungs switched back on.

When I heard the clomping of heavy feet behind me, I kicked into high gear. I ignored the screaming in my feet and I ran faster and faster until I was streaking through the shadows, branches whipping against my legs and face.

Young's footfalls hammered more faintly. Pulling away from him was better than all the Christmas presents I ever received. My blood sang with the joy of surviving. All those years of being chased, all that practice. Now it paid off. One more step and one more second and maybe I could hope to survive this night.

Then I tripped.

CHAPTER 40

I sprawled flat before I got my hands under me. My nose dug into the wet soil of someone's back yard. I smelled grass and fertilizer.

Hearing those thumping boots, I scrambled up. Pain flamed through my left ankle. Shuffling and hopping along, I tested it. It could handle a little weight, but my speed was cut in half.

I could not head for home. On the open street, I was easy prey. If I stretched my luck enough to get home, Rubino would probably be lurking.

No, I turned down a side street and headed for the woods. Like Brer Rabbit, I had to get to my briar patch.

I fled to the only place I felt safe. The lake. A sprained ankle meant nothing in water.

Once I was ten feet into the woods, all light snuffed out. Streetlights, houselights, and star glow disappeared. But I knew these woods. My feet found one of the game paths and I shuffled downhill. Toward the water. Always toward the water.

A branch raked across my face and brought a flood of tears into my eyes. I just kept them shut after that. I had to navigate the dark by feel, not sight.

The thrashing in the underbrush got closer.

I've been scared all kinds of times in my life, but this leaped off the charts. My guts felt like I had swallowed battery acid. A burning madness spread from my chest through my veins. I ran, but I felt my limbs twitching, like I barely had control. I couldn't think anymore. If the noise behind me had been a ravenous lion, I could not have felt more terrified. I measured my life in seconds.

My teeth hurt. The throbbing in my skull became the only thing I heard. My pulse raced faster and faster. I was reaching my limit. No, I had reached my limit earlier. I was now in uncharted territory.

My mother's voice spoke inside my head: "Jake, don't overdo it." The family doctor said, "Jake, don't overtax yourself. Sometimes your heart will try to pump too fast and you'll faint."

I was overdoing it far beyond anything I had ever overdone before. What should I do now? Stop? Listen to the doctor? Don't listen? Either way, in a minute I probably would be dead.

My left foot went wet to the ankle. I opened my eyes and saw the shimmer of reflected starlight off water. I'd reached the edge of the lake. As I tried to run into the shallows I sank knee-deep in soft mud. I clawed with my hands at tufts of grass that filled the marshy shallows, pulling forward, trying to get to open water. Shimmers of color danced across my vision. *No, please, dear God, do not let me faint. Please. I'll go to church this Sunday if you just let me live to see Sunday.*

Young grunted behind me. I heard the sucking sound as he pulled his feet clear of the mud. I heard his breath rasp out of his throat. It sounded like he was right on top of me. I dared not look back.

Grab. Pull. Move. I became a machine. Mud sucked at my feet, tore off my right sneaker. That helped a little. Less drag. If I had more time, I would have shucked off the other one.

Young's breath ripped in and out of him. I swore I could feel it on my wet skin. A bear chased me, or a bull, or the deadly Minotaur himself. That sound drove me mad because I could not get away from it.

"C'mere, ya little lyin' son of a bitch."

His fingers brushed against my calf. High voltage shot through me and colors closed in around the edges of my vision. My arms and legs flailed. He reached out again and his fingers clamped around my left foot. My leg spasmed so fast, Young wound up with my other sneaker as a prize.

A few more inches of water topped the mud now. I flopped forward and frantically kicked my feet to free them from the muck. If I could lay along the surface, I could slide along and shallow-swim over the mud until the water got deeper. Someone of Young's size would have to slog out much farther to begin swimming.

Pulling partly free of the ooze, I scrabbled forward, clawing along the mud surface like a salamander. I was slithering more than swimming, but Young's breathing seemed slightly farther back.

186

The water was maybe six inches on top of the mud, then a foot. If I had the breath, I would have yelled, I was so happy. Swimmable water. That bastard would never catch me now.

My head filled with visions of freedom.

That's when I felt Young's hand wrap around my right ankle.

CHAPTER 41

I screamed as that python grip tightened. I kicked and writhed and twisted like an eel as a sound like wind blew in my ears. In a few seconds I knew what would happen. I would go limp and fall into a faint from which I would never awaken.

Open water beckoned from just a few yards away. Freedom. In total panic mode, I flailed with my free leg. I think I hit him in the face. He grunted. I literally spun my entire body. Those fat fingers slid down my foot and I bolted.

I frog-kicked twice, then began an overhand racing stroke. Straight out I went, toward deep water, toward the inky black. As panic lessened just a notch and as the cooling water slid over my body, the color shimmers receded from my vision. In my element I had a chance.

Maybe I was feeling a little cocky because I didn't think Young could swim very fast in boots, so I turned to figure out where he was. I saw starlight glinting on ripples and I heard the churning of water. I was wrong. Young was maybe twenty feet behind and closing fast. Those massive arms were like oars. He didn't even need legs.

He couldn't possibly be catching me. I was a great swimmer. Yet I heard the crash of water coming closer. Panic engulfed me again.

Here was my shark, an implacable machine with only one goal. I knew what my father had experienced that night in the dark waters of the Pacific.

And I saw what he meant. I could go faster because I *had* to go faster. My willpower dictated the terms.

I think for a few seconds I barely touched the water. I swam like I had never swum. My arms arced forward and my legs snapped, just as my father had taught me. Every instruction I had ever been given for cutting through water with utmost efficiency rang in my head. Hands flat, toes extended.

The problem was the drag of my clothes. I kicked while my hands undid my belt buckle. It took a second to shed my cut-offs.

I porpoised straight up, gulped a breath and knifed straight down. I hit maybe ten feet below the surface and ripped off my T-shirt. I stayed down a long time. I heard Young kicking above me, so I swam at a tangent to the direction I had been going. Pull through the water, then glide. Then pull again, and glide. I heard a pounding roar, like a motorboat. I realized it was my pulse, hammering in my head, deafening me as my body screamed for air.

I cut to the surface. It took every bit of willpower I had to gently break into the air and to inhale quietly with my mouth wide open. I wanted to shovel oxygen into my lungs, but fear is a powerful motivator. I dared not give away my position by breathing hard. Night tag had trained me well.

It seemed like minutes went by before my breathing caught up to my oxygen starvation. While I breathed, I shucked off my underpants. I needed every advantage. Young was just too powerful a swimmer. I surveyed the water. Here and there, lights along the shore stretched out in little shimmering comet tails of illumination across the surface. I looked for any break in those lines caused by the disturbance of a swimmer. Nothing. Young had gone as silent as I was.

Slowly I rotated. There! I saw ripples.

I dropped down and pulled myself underwater, away from the disturbance on the surface. I traveled about fifty feet, slid my head above the surface and breathed.

As the water calmed me down, my brain started to work again. More lights shimmered across the water and I got my bearings.

Submerge, long stroke, glide. Stroke, then glide again. Surface quietly and breathe. Again. I don't know how long I did this, but I knew my life depended on doing it right. No game of night tag had ever tested my abilities to this extent. Sharon was right about swimming nude. I don't think I had ever cut through the water as fast as I did now. I imagined myself a torpedo slicing through the blackness with almost no drag at all.

Surfacing, I looked around and recognized lights on shore. I had come a long way, but when I saw where I was, I had an idea. Breast stroke. Stay low in the water. Minimum ripples.

I lined up two lights with a third. My right foot brushed against sand. I lowered my feet to my submerged island and rested for the first time in – how long? – fifteen minutes? It wasn't until I relaxed that I realized how tired I was. I needed this rest. Let Young burn up his energy out there.

A hundred yards of water separated me from shore. I was a tiny speck of darkness in a great blob of darkness. I could rest and watch from my little submerged island, like when I played water tag. I felt more hopeful that I could get away. I just had to be patient.

A tiny ripple cut across a light beam. It seemed like nothing. Surely not a man. Oh, great, what if a water moccasin came at me? I was terrified of those things. One bite and I might as well just go under and drown. I'd be dead before I could reach the shore.

The hand that suddenly clutched my neck felt as cold as the water. It sent an electric shock through me that saved my life because I jerked so hard, I broke free. Filling my lungs, I went down. My hands swept around madly as I tried to find the boulder that I knew was out here. With a lungful of air, I would bob to the surface unless I had something to weigh me down. It took an eternity before I rapped my knuckles against the pitted rock. Grabbing on, I planted my feet in the sand and crouched as low as I could. If I stayed stationary, Young might think I had swum off and go looking. I had to wait. Hold my breath as long as possible and wait.

How had Young stayed with me? Was he that much better than me? I remembered what Munson had told me about Young and Rubino in the war. They weren't just regular Army, they were Rangers. Super-trained killing machines. Probably jungle fighters. Probably took on half of Tojo's army single-handed.

It dawned on me that maybe Young hadn't followed me. Maybe he had swum straight for my house, assuming that a panicked boy would head for home. Maybe he had just been treading water in the cove waiting for me to show up. I wouldn't have time to consider it further.

A foot crashed into my head. I yelped and lost half my air.

I don't know what made me do what I did next. I reached out with my left hand and felt around above me. My fingers brushed against cloth. I closed my fist on his pants and pulled. The leg kicked, but I kept pulling, my other hand firmly clutching a handhold in the rock.

Buddy Young didn't know he could stand. He thrashed to stay above water, expending energy as I held on.

His free leg smashed into my face, half stunning me, but I maintained my grip. I pulled with all my strength. The black water churned. I kept my eyes closed. There was nothing to see, but plenty to hear: Young's muffled voice screaming under the surface; his arms and legs thrashing through the water; my heart thundering in my ears as my air got used up.

My lungs flamed now, but Young struggled on. My fingers gripped the boulder so hard, they went numb.

Something in me snapped. *You bastard,* was all I could think. *You killed your daughter. You used her like a whore and you killed her. And you cut out her eyes. Why did you do that? Because she looked at you funny? You filthy bastard. Die already. Just die, Goddammit! Die! DIE!*

I thought of Munson. "You can't take the law into your own hands."

Wrong, Lieutenant. Right now, I do hold the law in my hands. And I will hold onto this pant leg and this rock until this lake freezes over next winter if I have to.

I was prepared to drown, if it meant stopping this bastard. Oh, God, how I hated him.

It doesn't take much weight to sink a swimmer. Anchored to the boulder, I had the advantage. Young being drunk also helped.

I don't know what happened. Maybe he got tired. Maybe I yanked unexpectedly and he inhaled a mouthful of water. That's all it takes. One mouthful in the lungs, you start to cough, you inhale, and it's all over. Two years ago, I had seen Bobby Nelson try to save his brother, just twenty feet from shore. Bobby was on the swim team, a strong swimmer, but that didn't mean anything when his little brother, Billy, panicked and grabbed onto Bobby and wouldn't let go. The police dredged them both up on the ends of grappling hooks an hour later.

192

Maybe Young just gave up, weighed down by his guilt. Whatever the reason, Buddy Young's legs stopped kicking.

Then I suspected a trick. He was an army ranger. How could a hundred pounds of me drown two hundred pounds of him? I held onto his pants as the fire built in my lungs. How long had it been since I breathed?

The weight of Young's boots dragged him down and his bulk thumped against me like a big rubber mannequin. I emptied my lungs with a scream loud enough to knock fish unconscious. I jumped so hard I flew halfway out of the lake.

I swore it was a trick. Somehow I had made a mistake and his banana fingers would be twisting through the blackness and grab me and I would breathe water, not air. I frothed into a speed stroke and sped straight for my beach. As I dragged myself out of the water, I turned and listened. I didn't hear anything but the tiny lapping of ripples against the sand.

How was he not behind me? My heart hammered like crazy. All the panic came back. I ran up the hill, but I didn't make it to my house. Halfway up I got dizzy and sprawled onto the damp grass. I think I fainted because I suddenly didn't know where I was. Why was I lying naked in my back yard?

Then I remembered and sat up, ready to run away. I listened for splashing or footsteps or breathing. Other than insects, I didn't hear anything. If he was alive, Buddy Young should be right behind me, hulking up the hill like Frankenstein.

Now I knew for sure. He hadn't been faking.

He was dead and I had killed him. I had wanted him dead, but wanting it and actually doing it are worlds apart.

As warm as the night was, I started to shiver. Another body drifted in the lake. More boats and grappling hooks. Police. But this time they'd come for me too. I had sunk so deep in the crap that I would never get out.

I hobbled up the hill. My left ankle hurt, but not as badly as right after I fell. That seemed a long time ago. I slumped onto a bench and leaned forward on the picnic table, drinking in the air, letting me heart slow. I rested for a few minutes and then headed for the back door.

Before I opened the door, I stopped. If I went inside, a whole string of events would start. My parents would ask questions, the police would be called, and they'd ask questions. Munson would arrive and I just couldn't stand the way he would look at me. If I went into my house, I'd never get out again.

Meanwhile, what about Sharon and Ralph?

I listened to the night sounds. I didn't hear sirens. As I thought back, I couldn't remember hearing sirens while I was in the lake. Nobody had called the police. So, Sharon could still be tied to her bed and Ralph could be unconscious on the floor.

Or dead. Nobody knew that anything had happened.

I should call the police. An ambulance should go to Sharon's house, but it would take time. I could be at Sharon's house before I would even finish a phone call.

I stepped around the side of my house and thanked all gods that my mother had not brought in the laundry. I dressed in dry clothes: underwear, T-shirt, cut-offs, my summer uniform. It felt wonderful to not be clammy anymore. I had no shoes, but with all the time I spent barefoot, the bottoms of my feet had hardened to leather.

Trotting as fast as I could up the street, I dreaded what I would find.

CHAPTER 42

I was so out of breath when I got there, I could barely scale the front steps. My body had never been taxed as it had been in the hours since Rubino chased me. My poor little heart. My mother would surely say I was overdoing it.

I staggered across the front porch and tore open the screen door. Frantically, I sped through the living room. A dark pool of Ralph's blood glistened on the oak floor, but Ralph had disappeared. The house maintained an unnerving silence, like it was alive and holding its breath. I hustled up the stairs. When I came to Sharon's room, I stopped in my tracks. I wanted to retch.

She was still spread-eagled across her bed, her hands and feet still tied to the bed frame. Tendons stood out on her neck as she strained to raise her head. Her eyes flashed like a wild animal. "It's okay," I said. I rushed to the side of the bed and started to untie her left arm. Sharon's head rocked from side to side and noise came out of her throat. "It's okay. I'll have you out of here in no time." She squirmed like crazy.

If I hadn't just come through the ordeal of my life, I might have noticed that when I left her, she had talked to me. Now she was gagged. If I hadn't been so interested in her bindings, I might have seen sooner that her eyes did not focus on me. They stared behind me. I turned just as fireworks erupted in my head and darkness dropped on me like a blanket.

* * *

With lazy strokes, I swam through warm, murky fluid and slowly rose to the light of the surface. When I broke through, I gasped and sucked in air.

Ralph Young's bloody face loomed over me as he straddled my body. His hands held a Louisville Slugger. "Jake, you should be more careful. You tripped and hit your head." The laugh that rattled out of him made me want to be unconscious again.

My thoughts swirled. What was happening? "Ralph?" I managed to croak.

"It's too bad you were so obsessed with my sister. Hounding Sharon like that. Bad mojo. Too bad I caught you and you attacked me. Too bad I had to beat you with a bat. Too bad you died."

"Ralph, take it easy. What's going on here?"

"Why should I tell you?"

"Untie your sister." The force in my voice surprised even me.

"Oh, no. She's where she needs to be. By the way, where's my bastard of a father?"

I spat it out. "Drowned."

Ralph's face lit up. I saw the gears working. Maybe he was less stupid than I always thought. He sat on my chest and stroked the bat against my cheek.

"That's interesting, Jake. The old bastard's dead?"

Something moved off to the side, but I didn't turn my head. I concentrated on peripheral vision. I had loosened her bindings enough that Sharon was able to get her left arm free. She worked on her other hand. I had to keep Ralph occupied.

I said, "Yeah, and I called the police. They'll be here any minute, so you might as well let me go."

Sharon's right arm came free.

"I'm having too much fun. Isn't that right, Sis? It's a fun evening. A family party." He started to look over his shoulder. She froze.

I struggled enough to make Ralph look back at me. "It's over, Ralph. Why are you doing this?"

"You think you're so damn smart, don't you, Little Sherlock? You don't know crap."

Sharon's left leg was free. Just one to go. I had to keep Ralph talking.

"That's right. I don't know crap. You're the expert on crap, aren't you, Ralph?"

His eyes flared. "The most important crap right now, Jakey, is that my old man didn't kill my sister."

He smiled at the shock on my face.

"Never saw that coming, did you, you little barfbag..."

Ralph didn't see what was coming either. Sharon picked up a glass snow globe from her bureau. In two quick steps, she stood above Ralph. Her teeth jammed together in a grimace and she slammed the globe down on Ralph's head so hard I heard his skull pop.

Ralph's weight dropped on me like a sand bag. His face slammed into my left cheek. I heard a gurgling hiss as his breath escaped. He didn't breathe in. I smelled the sourness of his armpits.

"Get him off me!" I struggled under the limp weight. Sharon heaved on his shoulder and he rolled off. He came to rest half on his side, blank eyes staring at the middle of my chest. Between us the snow globe rested on the floor, snowflakes swirling around a tiny village with a church and decorated Christmas trees.

I sat up not believing I was alive. Sharon perched on the edge of the bed and pulled the top sheet around her naked body. Her eyes didn't focus. She said, "*He* killed Janey. I thought my dad did it." She shook her head.

I scrabbled backwards, away from this new corpse, until my back hit the wall. Ralph killed Janey? My brain couldn't handle this new information. Too many bodies dropping. Too many gears to shift. "We need to call the police."

"You said you did already."

"No. I just wanted to scare Ralph."

She stared at me. "How did my father die?"

"In the lake. He followed me out into the middle." I couldn't tell her the rest.

"How do you know he's dead?"

"I heard him struggling. He went down and he didn't come back up."

She looked right through me. I knew she saw the lie. I wanted to vomit. I opened my mouth to admit it, yes, I killed him, but she spoke first.

"Good. I'm glad he's dead. Filthy pervert."

She leaned forward and sobbed. I crawled to my feet and sat next to her. When I put my hand on her shoulder, she jerked. "Don't touch me."

"I'm sorry. I thought..."

"I don't want anyone touching me." She looked up and spat on her brother's body. "Filthy prick bastard. I hope he rots in hell for killing my sister."

"Ralph ...?"

She peered up at me with bloodshot eyes. "Jake, you don't understand what went on in this house. For years my father made me have sex with him. Ralph thought he'd have a try. He tied me to my bed. My father thought I was his private property. When he found Ralph up here tonight, he beat him senseless. Only Daddy was supposed to be able to screw his little princesses." She lowered her head as if all her energy was now expended.

"Janey too?"

"Yes, Janey too!"

I settled back on the floor and leaned against the wall. She radiated a weird energy. Being close to her felt creepy.

"Why would Ralph kill Janey?"

Her voice almost whispered. "A few months ago, Ralph started forcing her to have sex with him. I guess he figured if Dad could do it, why couldn't he? He got her pregnant. She threatened Ralph that if he didn't leave her alone, she would tell Dad it was Ralph's. Dad would have killed him. The only reason he didn't tonight was because you showed up and he chased after you."

"So, all Ralph had to do was leave Janey alone. He didn't need to kill her."

"Maybe he didn't trust her to keep her mouth shut when the baby arrived. Maybe he did it for spite. He hated our father. Took away his prized possession. I don't know. Maybe he did it because he had a screw loose. Try getting the snot kicked out of you every week, Jake. See if that affects your judgement."

She squinted at me. "How are your clothes dry?"

"I got them off the clothesline at my house."

"Anyone see you?"

"No."

She stared into space for a few seconds.

"Jake, just go home."

"What? But the police..."

"I'll tell them Ralph attacked me and I fought him off. You don't even need to get involved. I'm the one who hit him with the paperweight."

"But your father and Janey, what...?"

"I'll tell them Ralph drowned my father and boasted about it to me. He killed my sister. He was about to kill me. It all holds together. He was a nut job. Nobody to dispute it. And he had a juvie record. The police will be happy to shut the case. No need for you to get dragged through the mud."

"But what do I say?"

"You go home and you don't say anything. It's simple. Just keep your mouth shut."

"But..."

"You said it all a few minutes ago. It's over. Let's not make it complicated. Just go."

She lowered her head. "Go out the back door and cut across the yard. Better if nobody sees you coming out the front door."

I trudged home in a trance. In less than an hour, I had helped kill two people.

CHAPTER 43

I crept into my house through the basement door, checked my workbench clock. 11:14. Standing frozen at the foot of the stairs, I listened. No floorboards creaked. No voices. No television.

Was this my only good luck of the day? With all that had happened, would I just stroll into my house and go to bed?

I climbed the stairs slowly, keeping my feet along the sides of the treads to avoid causing a squeak. I rotated the knob of the door at the top of the stairs and pushed. The light above the kitchen sink provided the only illumination on the main floor. I turned my head back and forth, trying to sense if anyone was up. The scents of dinner lingered in the air: fried chicken, vinegar, coffee.

I turned the corner and crossed the living room. One more corner and up the stairs and I'd be in my room. Sleeping on the porch was out of the question. Opening the sofa bed would cause too much noise. I let out my breath.

"You're in trouble, young man."

Until that moment I had thought ice water in the veins was a lousy metaphor, but I suddenly knew what it meant. I felt like my body had entered a meat locker.

My brain processed for two seconds and came up with a brilliant response. "Mom?"

My mother sat in a stuffed chair, with only the right side of her face lit by a streetlight through the window. How did she know? Had she seen me come up from the lake and change my clothes?

"Where were you all day?"

Oh, it was a mom-trap. She already knew, but she wanted to test me. If I said something different, I was dead. If I confirmed what she knew, I was dead. Might as well just order the flowers.

"I'm sorry. I called you."

"Sorry? What are you doing coming in after eleven? Curfew is ten."

"It's summer, Mom."

"You said you were staying with Eddie. I called his house. His mother said you hadn't been there all evening. I can't go to sleep if I know you're out somewhere. I worry. Why do you do this to me?"

She didn't know. She was pissed that I was out late. That was all. She had no idea what had happened in the lake. It would be better if she did know. It would feel better to be punished than to harbor my terrible secret. I wanted to crawl away from her eyes and get under a rock.

"I'm sorry, Mom."

"You lied. No allowance for two weeks." She rose and drifted through the shadows toward her bedroom.

CHAPTER 44
July 25, 1965

I slept until noon, most unusual for me. They say the guilty wear themselves out with their burden.

I trudged down the stairs from my room.

"Jake, c'mere," Paul shouted.

He lay sprawled across a chair on the back porch, staring at the lake. Beyond him, through the screens, I saw a half dozen motorboats trolling across the far side of the lake, strung out side-by-side in a jagged line. Motorboats were not allowed on the lake. It had to be the police. Sharon had told her story and the endgame had begun.

I hunched in another chair and watched the slow progression. "They've been out since early this morning," Paul said, his voice tinged with awe. "There's gonna be a body. Maybe more."

Yes, there certainly would be a body.

I didn't feel hungry. I just sat with my little brother and watched the boats. Yellow nylon ropes hung over their sterns on metal frames that kept the lines away from the propellers. From when I had seen them deployed to find Janey Young's body, I knew that each line held a grappling hook big enough to catch Moby Dick. Big lead weights kept them down.

They trolled in the wrong place. I could have told them exactly where to drag. I could have gone down there and dived into the water and come up with Buddy Young's body in three minutes.

Yet I didn't.

It's a big lake. They took all day running their grid search.

My parents came home from work and Paul went crazy telling them about the boats. His tongue machine-gunned details and commentary as we all sat on the back porch and watched the search. We were a perfect portrait of family togetherness. A warm and fuzzy moment that could last until they took me away and locked me up.

A beacon radiated out of my head, shining into the sky like the bat signal. Here I am! It's me! I did it!

My mother made dinner and everyone ate but me. The slow unfolding grid pattern of the boats hypnotized me. I imagined this was how it felt just before the guillotine came down. You know what's going to happen. You know it's the end of you, but you're powerless to change the outcome.

The sun dropped below the horizon and the police boats turned on spotlights. I knew something had happened by the way all the boats suddenly jammed together. Paul, who had wolfed down his dinner and returned to his post, ran to get our parents. This was better than the World Series for him.

They pulled the body onto the public beach on the far side of the lake. Flashing lights. People milling around. Paul got his binoculars and stayed glued to the window.

"Holy cow, it looks like a whale on the beach."

"Paul, show some respect."

"For what, Mom? It's some big guy we don't even know."

How long before we would hear a knock at the door?

The story hit the news and created another media circus. Teen Girl Fights Off Murderous Brother. Lakeview Lunatic. Horror Hits Lakeview. On and on. The township police chief shook hands with the township mayor on the front page of the local paper, as if either one had anything to do with solving the case.

No mention of Little Sherlock. Thankfully, my shelf life had expired. Or so I hoped.

My nerves had burnt out. My hands shook. I shuffled like an old man. My body hurt in so many places I had to sneak aspirins out of the medicine cabinet just to get through the day.

Every waking second I expected the police to smash down the front door to drag me away. I sat on the sofa in the living room and stared at the TV hour after hour. I can't remember a single thing I saw.

Arguments started inside my head. Condemnations followed by long, complex justifications.

I killed a man.

But he had been trying to kill me. What else could I do in that situation? He was a dirt bag who beat and raped his daughters.

But it was wrong to kill. I could have swum away in the dark. Instead, I waited for him. I ambushed him. And in those final moments the only thing in the world I wanted was Buddy Young to be dead. I had screamed it in my head. I was a killer.

And Ralph? Sharon smashed his skull, not me. An accident. Yeah, but I had let her creep up on him. That was my participation. But Ralph intended to kill me too. Father and son, both wanted me dead. What had I done to deserve it? Everything that had happened was merely justice. Why should I feel bad?

Then back to feeling even more disgusted with myself. The vicious circle tightened around me like a noose.

I thought of going to church and confessing to a priest. "Bless me, Father, for I have sinned. I used the Lord's name in vain three times. I had impure thoughts six times. I talked back to my mother once. Oh, yes, and yesterday I killed two people." The poor priest might have a stroke.

A priest couldn't break a confession confidence, could he? Wouldn't God strike him dead if he did? Like in the Bible: "God smote him down."

I thought if God decided that anyone needed smoting, I was the most likely smotation target. I should not go anywhere near a church or God might notice me. Best to stay under God's radar.

I didn't dare call Munson. He should think about me even less than God.

The next morning, the doorbell rang. I froze. I had expected it, but now I couldn't believe it. My parents were at work and I hadn't seen Paul. I had to face justice alone. The doorbell rang again. My visitor was impatient.

I could have just sat. I could have ignored it, but I went to a front window and peeked through the curtains.

Munson.

My feet moved of their own will. My hand opened the door. It seemed funny how the past couple days my body parts acted on their own with me merely observing.

A whiff of Old Spice aftershave. "Hey, Sherlock."

"Lieutenant."

"Well, Jake, looks like Sharon Young saved the state the cost of a trial. That brother. What a piece of work."

Sharon's story had held together, just as she said it would.

I don't know what expression my face held, but it prompted Munson to say, "Jake, are you okay?"

I couldn't tell him I hurt inside like pieces of me had shattered. "Why did you come to my house?"

"I wanted to thank you personally for your help. And to tell you I talked to my captain about Rubino almost running you down with his cruiser. He sliced Rubino a brand new asshole. He won't bother you anymore. And if his daughter tries anything, she's looking at a battery charge. You don't have to spend the next five years in your yard." He smiled.

No, I should spend twenty-five to life in the state's yard.

So, in twenty-four hours the number of people who would whip my ass on sight was down by two thirds: Rubino, Rubino's daughter, Buddy Young, and Ralph Young. That left Carl and Animal. In comparison, they hardly seemed like problems.

"That's great, Lieutenant."

"You don't seem happy."

He hadn't come to slap cuffs on me. I was free, just as Sharon said I'd be, but I didn't feel any better about it.

"Just worn out. It's been a bad couple weeks."

"Yeah, you've seen more than a kid should see." He turned toward his car. When he was halfway there, he said over his shoulder, "What I said about coming to see me after you graduate, I meant it. Give it some thought. You have a talent."

Yeah. A talent for trouble.

CHAPTER 47
July 31, 1965

Day five. Sharon called. "Can you come over?"

"Yeah, when?"

"In a half hour?"

"Okay." Why did I say that? How bad was *this* idea?

Staring at the kitchen wall clock made the time go more slowly, but not slowly enough. I don't think a single thought slid through my head as I watched the sweep hand lurch from dot to dot. Finally, it was time for me to lurch out the front door. The mid-day heat rippled off the street and blurred anything in the distance. It felt like walking through a pizza oven. Good practice for hell.

My guts squirmed at the prospect of being anywhere near the Young house. As it loomed out of the heat haze, I slowed my steps. How could I possibly go back inside that place? Only the prospect of seeing Sharon kept my feet moving.

A For Sale sign on her front lawn jolted panic through my veins. She was moving? I mounted the steps and lifted the door knocker. Before I could drop it, the door swung open. Sharon must have watched for my arrival.

"Hello, Jake. Come on in." Her smile seemed brittle and tight. She wore a sky-blue dress and white tennis shoes that set off her tan beautifully. That little dress barely dropped to the middle of her thighs. I'd never seen such sheer material. It left nothing to the imagination, like she was naked but with clothes on.

"Your house is for sale?" I could think of nothing else to say. I mean, what options did I have? Hi, how are things since I killed your father?

"Can't keep this place, Jake. Too many bad memories to deal with." She half-smiled. "They were cremated this morning. Both of them. I'm free now."

It was slipping away from me. She suddenly looked so much older. Generations older. I was just a kid entering puberty. She was a woman and I never had the slightest chance with her. I wanted to drip through the floorboards and sink into the earth.

She pulled me to her and wrapped her arms around me. That hot skin-in-the-sun scent wafted off her body. Her hair held the fragrance of peaches. I was surprised my skin wasn't tingling where her chest pressed against me. Last week it would have.

I rested my face against her neck for a moment. Her skin felt hot and I heard the strong pulse of her. She pushed me back and held my shoulders at arm's length and cocked her head to one side. "This is good-bye, Jake."

It all happened too fast. My head started spinning. I flopped onto the couch.

"Poor baby. I know it's sudden, but it's for the best."

"But what do I do? The police? I, I just…"

"Don't worry about the police. It's all finished. I didn't mention your name. Nobody will ever bother you."

I said, "Except my conscience." I felt like an animal with a bear trap around my ankle, thinking of gnawing off my own foot.

"You helped me. You did nothing wrong, Jake."

"Yeah, I did."

She settled next to me, but said nothing, her tawny eyes gazing expectantly into mine. Her eyes seemed so clear I wondered if they were real.

I said, "I told you your father drowned, but that was only half true. I pulled him under. I thought *he* was a murderer. But now I am."

She pressed her right index finger against my lips. "No more, Jake. No more secrets. That's over now."

"I have to tell the police."

A car horn beeped from the street. Three fast taps. Sharon glided to the far side of the room and leaned over to pick up a canvas tote bag. She set it next to my end of the sofa. "I'll be back in a minute." She disappeared down the hall, then the stairs creaked.

As I stared at the dark television screen, a horrible numbness spread through me. How many shocks could my system take before they put me in a rubber room? The past few weeks seemed like an endless stream of crises.

My gaze wandered across the living room. The dark stain in the oak, where Young had beaten his son to the floor, looked no different than the other stains in the floor. It could have been a hundred years old. Everything seemed tidy. Had Sharon cleaned the house? It seemed a strange thing to do, to clean a place and leave it.

The TV rested on a low bookshelf. At the bottom of the bookshelf a stack of newspapers stood a foot high. Why did my eyes keep going back to that stack? I drifted over to them, picked up the top paper. Ink smudged along the middle of the first page, the same way our paper looked at home. The paperboy wrapped a rubber band around the rolled up paper to make it easy for him to throw onto porches. When you pulled off the rubber band, it always smeared a little area of the front page.

I lifted a few more papers. They all had that little smear. At the rear of the shelf above the papers, a pile of red rubber bands peeked from behind a cigar box. They looked just like the ones we threw in the junk drawer at my house every day. Little black smudges on them from the newspaper ink.

Sharon had told me they didn't get the newspaper after I asked if she'd seen the Little Sherlock article.

Why lie about getting the newspaper?

As I returned to the sofa, my foot brushed against her canvas tote. I stared at it for several seconds. A little bell rang in the back of my head. Something didn't add up.

I reached into Sharon's canvas tote and moved things around. I saw a purse, some cosmetics. At the bottom of the bag was one of those homework notebooks with the marbled black and white covers. I pulled it out. When I saw the name on the cover my breath caught in my throat: Janey Young. On the line below: Diary 1965. I glanced down the hall as I opened the notebook, flipped through until I hit blank pages, backtracked. Janey's last entry. June 30. "I'll tell him tonight."

Tell who? Tell him what?

Then a line that threw my brain into a frenzy. "But before that, I have to do something really horrible. I have to tell Sharon my plans."

I backtracked more. I saw lots of references to CJ. Who was CJ? I couldn't think of anybody with those initials.

I heard water running upstairs. Scanned back over June, then May. If I heard footsteps, I would have to slam this thing back into the tote and put on my best poker face.

May 25: "My period is three days late. Oh, I hope I'm pregnant. But I can't tell CJ yet. Have to be sure. Have to miss two in a row."

I heard the upstairs toilet flush. Now I was on zero time. It was like that last few seconds during final exams when answers are dancing in your head, but you can only write so fast, and you're not finished, but the clock says you *will* be finished in seven, six, five…

I scanned as much as I could. Bat-boy hearing kicked in. The soft impacts of Sharon's tennis shoes drummed on the staircase. Five steps, six. I pushed the notebook back into the tote and stood it upright. The tone of her footfalls changed as her feet hit the oak flooring. Three steps. She was in the hall. No time even to sit up. I twisted slightly and tied my shoe as camouflage.

When I sat up, she stood in front of me. On the floor next to her she dropped a tweed overnight case, brown and tan. Fibers stuck out around the scuffed leather corners like this thing had seen a lot of places. It looked older than both our ages combined.

"Where are you going?"

"As far from here as I can get." Her face twisted in a way I had never seen before.

Just like in final exams, my mind swirled, but the importance of finals paled in comparison to this situation. Something had veered into the wrong lane. I just couldn't see it. Why did she have her sister's diary? It proved that her sister didn't commit suicide. It showed Janey knew of her pregnancy and that she told the baby's father the night she disappeared. She named the father. No mention of her brother Ralph. Who was CJ? Why hadn't Sharon given the diary to the police?

She had lied about the newspapers. A tiny thing. But why? Someone who would lie about a tiny thing would lie about a big thing. What was the bigger lie, the bigger pattern?

Out front a car horn honked again. Once, twice, then a long blast. I stood up. Sharon reached for the suitcase. Through the front windows I saw a red Corvette. Saw the guy in it. Chaz.

The swirling in my head slowed a little. Chaz-screw-'em-in-the-backseat-Dougal? It hit me hard. I hadn't seen the obvious.

I stared at Sharon. "Chaz? You're running off with Chaz? He'll dump you in a week."

Half a smile crept across her face. The other half I couldn't put a name to. "No, he's going to marry me." Unconsciously, her free hand went to her stomach. Just for an instant.

What had Chaz said to me that night? Why would Chaz break his own rules? Why would he marry a girl he considered nothing more than a piece of ass? The swirling stopped. In that moment I saw the larger pattern. Her hand going to her stomach. Yes.

"You're pregnant," I said.

Sharon's eyes widened for a fraction of a second. "How did you...?"

I gave her steel eye.

"Chaz got you pregnant." I said it like a robot.

She smiled. "I wanted Chaz to get me pregnant."

I'd wipe that smile off her face. "Was that before or after he got your sister pregnant?"

Yeah, the smile disappeared, wiped away by Jake, the vengeful little ferret. I hated her now.

"Stop making things up. You're being mean."

"I'm not making anything up. It's right there in her diary." I pointed at the tote bag.

Everyone had used the name Chaz for so long, I forgot that when we were really young, before he was a tough guy, he was nicknamed using his first two initials because his name was so damn long. Charles J. Dougal, Jr. became CJ.

"How the hell do you...?" She glanced down at the tote. "You sneaky little turd."

"Why would you let the police think your sister might have committed suicide? That book gives Chaz a pretty good motive."

She pondered for a moment. "You want to know? I fell in love with Chaz the first time I saw him. I did anything he wanted. He was mine, so my older sister had to have him. She didn't care about him. She stole everything from me for as long as I can remember. Chaz was my ticket out of here, so she stole him from me too. If I gave the police her diary, they would have gone after Chaz. I couldn't take that chance."

She gave me a look I hadn't seen before. Something dark and elusive flitted across those golden eyes.

Chaz was the logical person to have killed Janey. But it wasn't in Chaz's nature to do something like that.

If it wasn't Chaz and it wasn't Buddy Young? But she had told me Ralph had killed Janey. If that were true, she wouldn't have needed to protect Chaz. So, she lied. Again.

I remembered the line in Janey's diary. Janey had to do something horrible. She had to tell her sister. The last tumbler clicked into place. "When Ralph said his father didn't kill Janey, Ralph wasn't confessing. He meant that *you* killed your sister."

It caught her by surprise. She went silent for several seconds. In a soft voice she said, "I told you, Jake. There were too many secrets."

Something deep in her eyes stirred. Those eyes that I had thought so warm now looked like those of Kendall's Gila monsters. What had I done? My goddamn big mouth.

Her head tilted left and I knew what a mouse feels like when it faces a cat. Rip, crunch, then bye-bye. I knew what she was thinking.

"Sharon, you wouldn't be able to explain me away. Not now. Lieutenant Munson would figure it out."

Was her brain calculating the odds, examining all the angles? I must have been too much of a gamble because her eyes shifted. The moment passed. I breathed again.

My skin chilled. "I was wrong about your father."

Her eyes flashed. "No you weren't. He was a monster. He would have killed you."

"And what about Ralph?"

"He knew what happened. He followed Janey and me to the cliffs. He made me have sex or he was going to call the police on me."

"But I helped you out there too, with Ralph."

She shrugged. "You came along at the right time."

"But you were tied up in your bedroom. That couldn't have been staged for you to set up Ralph. You didn't know I'd be at your house that night."

Her gaze lowered. Her voice got small, just above a whisper. "I told you he *made* me do it with him. He'd overpower me and tie me up. When he was finished he'd say, 'What's the big deal? You can't get pregnant twice.' I hated him more than my father." She looked at me, her face splotchy and contorted. "I was his little *sister*. He was supposed to protect me."

Ralph. Poaching on the old man's private reserve. It got him killed. I blundered into the situation and changed the equation, but the outcome was the same. Whether Sharon or Buddy Young did it, that night Ralph's number was up.

I had to know one thing. "How did you kill her?"

That something came back into her eyes, like storm clouds crossing the sun. Something best left alone, but I had opened the box. I was surprised when she answered.

She stared over my shoulder. "For almost a year, we talked about leaving home. But we had no money; Janey didn't have a diploma. We thought we might get jobs as waitresses and somehow make ends meet. But we knew he'd look for us. He'd want us back."

"Your father."

"Yes. And if he found us, it would be worse than before. We went for a walk to talk about what we should do. At least I thought that was what we were going to talk about. Janey took me away from the house, down to the lake. We were on the cliffs where the swallows have nests. The sun had just set and we sat on a cliff with our feet dangling over the edge, watching the view. I couldn't figure why she took me so far. Then I realized why. She didn't want me losing it where anybody could hear me."

"Losing it about what?"

"She told me she was getting out, but she couldn't take me. I was stunned. Or, I thought I was stunned. I found out what being stunned was really like when she told me she was leaving with Chaz. I almost fell off the cliff. But even that was nothing compared to what she said next."

CHAPTER 48

"She said she was pregnant with Chaz's child."

"And you were pregnant too?"

"I had just found out the day before. My big sister was taking everything from me and leaving me to face my father. Once he found out I was pregnant, he'd probably kill me."

"So, what happened?"

"I pushed her off the cliff."

She said it so matter-of-factly, I didn't think I heard it right. Funny how my mind works. I should've been terrified, but instead, I was curious.

"Your father thought Ralph killed Janey?"

"He was a stupid bastard."

"So, why didn't he kill Ralph if he thought that?"

A smile twisted her mouth. "I don't know. Maybe he wanted Ralph to carry on the family name. Such a noble name."

I thought of the rubber bands, the newspapers, her lie. As soon as she'd seen the Little Sherlock article she came to my house to find out what I told the police. To see if there was anything that put her in danger. She could pump me better by playing dumb. Oh, she was quite an actress.

I thought of how fast she had shifted gears after smashing Ralph's skull. Instantly, she had a story of how he had gotten his sister pregnant and killed her. Her talent was scary. I was so outclassed.

"I could turn you in." I knew it was lame as soon as I said it.

"Jake, you're smarter than that. You have no proof. And you'd have to tell how you killed my father." Her gaze darted around the room. Her brain jumped from thought to thought like a gazelle. She nodded to herself like she had a revelation. She held up Janey's diary. "Then there's this. You'd be sending an innocent man to jail."

Now she had me big time. Totally outclassed.

She said it just to be sure I got the point, but she said it slowly, jerkingly as she worked out the details. "CJ gets Janey pregnant. She drops the bomb on him June thirtieth. It's right in her diary. She's going to tell him that night." Her eyes blazed. "I would testify that Chaz picked her up that night and I heard them arguing in the car. She never came home that night. You find her body the next day. Neat little ribbon." She nodded as she tied that ribbon in her mind.

"You told the police Ralph killed Janey."

"I told them Ralph *said* he killed Janey. I didn't see it."

"Why would Ralph admit to killing his sister if Chaz had done it?" I asked.

Her eyeballs twitched back and forth as if she was seeing it all unfold before her. "I'd tell them Ralph wanted to scare me, control me, make me think he'd kill me too if I didn't have sex with him. How could I have known he was lying just so he could use me?"

"Don't you think the police would be suspicious that you didn't tell them about your sister's supposed argument with Chaz?"

She was leaning back and forth, like a boxer warming up. "I never mentioned it because by then Ralph admitted he was the killer. Later, when I found the diary and figured out it was Chaz, I tell them I was afraid. That Chaz threatened me. He knew I'd seen him pick up Janey. He knew I was the only one who could cause him trouble."

"He might kill you too to keep you quiet. Why would the cops believe you ran off with him?"

She was picking up the thread of her story more easily, weaving it into whole cloth. "I'd tell them he made me do it so he could control me and prevent me from telling the truth. What could I do? With my father dead, I have no way to support myself. Selling the house will barely cover my father's debts. I'm just a seventeen-year-old girl, Jake. Chaz is a big, strong man. I don't know what to do. I go with him out of confusion and fear. He tells me that he killed Janey. He tells me he won't hurt me if I'm good to him, do what he wants. The police would eat it up."

Her voice had been halting at times, but now she saw the conclusion of her concoction and she finished strong. "They'd have Chaz not just on the murder, but also for

218

kidnapping me. I'm pregnant because of him. You see, Jake, if you open your mouth, what's in the diary comes out and it's the electric chair for Chaz. You'd be killing an innocent man. But you're already good at killing, aren't you?"

Sledge hammers pounded every inch of my flesh. My little world crashed into the sun.

She held up the diary. "This is my get-out-of-jail-free card. And if Chaz ever thinks of dumping me, I'll tell him about it. The book goes in a safe deposit box. It sits there like a land mine. Everyone's safe as long as it's in there. If it ever comes out... Well, you can see how messy it would be. For you too."

She plopped the diary back in her bag. "Thank you for your sweet little confession, Jake. I promise never to tell anyone you drowned my father..." She lowered her head and peeked out from under her brows in a cutesy little girl look. "...unless I have to."

Chaz really laid on the horn this time.

"I have to go," she said.

"Why doesn't he come to the door?" I said. "Wouldn't a gentleman come to the door?"

"Chaz will never be a gentleman."

"Yeah, I guess you get what you deserve."

"You really are such a perfect little sweetie-pie. If I had more time, I'd just eat you right up."

Yeah, I thought. And pick your teeth with the bones.

She lifted the suitcase and the canvas tote and looked at me as if we only chatted about the weather. "Would you get the door?" We stepped from the gloomy interior of that dead house into burning sunshine. As she locked the door, I turned to examine Chaz. Sunglasses, big smile. The 'Vette's 327 engine idling with a sound like the bubbles make when you get water from a water cooler.

I watched those long legs lope down the steps. Her hard-muscled arms threw her meager luggage behind the bucket seat. Her hair fluffed above her in a weightless splash of sunlight as she hopped over the passenger door and landed with the skill of an acrobat. Her lips gave Chaz a kiss. Her eyes found me. She did not blink as her mouth worked on Chaz. Reptile eyes.

219

I remembered the day when I first met her, the day we spent together. I thought that had been real, before all the mess started, a glimpse of the person she might have become, but it was all a hoax.

I had always asked myself, why me? Why was I so lucky to have her become my friend? Now I understood why Sharon showed up at my beach that first day. She had seen my boat the evening she pushed her sister off the cliff. I was easy to track down. So, she got close to me to find out if I saw her on the cliffs with her sister. If I had recognized her, would I now be a corpse? She had gotten me into the most remote part of the lake on that first day, right near the cliffs. It had been a high-risk play on her part, putting me at the exact spot where my memory might be jogged. I shuddered when I thought of how close I had come to being drowned.

And when that stupid newspaper article said I was helping the police, she fed me information that deflected suspicion onto her father and brother.

Me. Sucker. From day one.

The tumblers in my head spun again and I saw the one thing that never made sense. Why had Rubino been so incensed about me trying to ruin his friend's life? I had assumed that somehow through the police department he found out what I told Munson.

No, just the reverse. He found out from Buddy Young and Young heard it from his daughter. Whatever I told Sharon got relayed to Buddy with probably a lot more that she made up. Made her father feel like I was digging his grave for a murder he knew he hadn't committed. No wonder he chased me.

Flipside, she told me things about her father that she knew I'd tell Munson, things that would throw more suspicion on Buddy Young. Anything to get him out of her life. She played both ends against the middle like a pro. Did she kill Pee-Wee too?

The temperature topped ninety-five in the shade. The humidity was about the same. Yet I was as cold as if five pounds of ice had suddenly appeared in my guts. I would never know the answers.

Yeah. Outclassed. Big time.

"Hey, Jake, what're you doin' here?" Chaz waved me down off the porch.

"Just sayin' good-bye, Chaz." I was surprised I could speak.

Sharon brightened up, got all bubbly. "Come here and give me a hug." She rose onto her knees on the seat. "C'mon."

Yeah, make a big deal. Show Chaz I'm just a kid from the neighborhood saying farewell. Nothing to make him suspicious.

I walked around to the passenger side. She grabbed at me like she was leaving on a long ocean voyage and I was the send-off party. Smiling. A fake hug like actors give each other at the Academy Awards. Even though her lips were only an inch from my ear, I barely heard what she whispered. "Jake, my father never raped us. It was Ralph. You had no reason to drown dear old dad. Remember that if you think about talking to your cop friend."

She dropped back onto the leather, not bothering to pull the perfect blue of that tiny dress down over the perfect golden skin of her thighs. Her eyes said it: take a last look, little boy. Then she waved frantically as if I were a hundred yards away. "Bye, Jake. Bye-bye."

I didn't wave. I didn't say a word.

I was a survivor of Hiroshima, or Nagasaki, or Mount Saint Helen, alive, but not sure if that was a good thing. I felt numbed from the blast wave that was Sharon Young. Had she hated her brother and father so much? She had directly or indirectly killed her whole family. I would never know why. I realized that everything I knew, or thought I knew, had come from Sharon. Every word. With everyone else gone, there was no way to find out what really happened in that house.

Was she lying again? Just to torment me? She was like a rabid animal, just clawing at everything around her, infecting everything with her disease and not caring. My brain spun into chaos.

A red Corvette convertible with a hot dog at the wheel, a pretty girl in the passenger seat, and more road than they could ever drive in front of them. It looked so perfect.

Chaz punched a button on his eight-track and Shorty Long started singing *Devil With The Blue Dress On.*

Yeah, Shorty, you got that right.

In a rumble of mufflers, she was gone.

Heat shimmered off the asphalt. When the 'Vette was three blocks away, it looked like it was gliding over water.

Something poked my arm and I almost jumped out of my sneakers. It was only Little Vinnie. He grinned up at me with buck teeth and the kind of horrible sunburn only redheads get. "Hey, Jake, can I buy some firecrackers?" He was short for twelve. One of my best customers. His right hand wrapped around a bunch of wadded up bills.

I looked back down the street at the fading mirage of Chaz's car. "I'm out of that business, Vinnie."

"Nothing left?"

"Come to my house after dinner. I'm making you the new Firecracker King."

"For how much?"

"Keep your money. It's a gift." Funny how fast you can shed an old skin.

I watched the red Corvette smudge into a blurred nothingness.

I stood there in the sun until my scalp practically melted.

The next morning I stayed in bed until I heard my parents leave for work. Then I put on real pants, and socks and shoes, all black. After two months of my being mostly barefoot, the shoes squeezed my toes. I picked out a short-sleeved denim shirt I really liked.

When I went downstairs, booger-boy looked up from his cereal. "Oooh, Jake must be going to see the naked girlfriend. Smoochy-smoochy."

I shot Paul a look that shut him up instantly. Even his rabid brain knew there were limits.

The bus trip downtown seemed to take about thirty seconds. I had hoped to collect my thoughts during the five mile ride, but suddenly the bus doors squeaked open and barfed me onto the sidewalk.

I shuffled along hot the concrete. I knew where I was going. I just didn't want to get there right away.

Three blocks. Then two.

I saw the pillars, the steps, the statues of City Hall. Police headquarters.

Lieutenant Munson would be inside. I imagined him sitting at some dingy old desk, with a cup of coffee in one hand and a cigarette in the other. No, he didn't smoke. Maybe just the coffee. Stale, crappy, cold instant coffee. Maybe like Mike Hammer he had a knockout secretary named Velda. Maybe he was cleaning his gun. He would look up, give me that raised-eyebrow look.

I wondered what look he would give me when I told him the whole story. I'd be in the headlines again. A lot. Little Sherlock Cracks Case, then, Little Sherlock Stands Trial. My only chance for getting life in prison was if my father didn't kill me first.

My right foot poised on the first wide marble step. The entrance seemed a long way off. It looked like I was about to climb the great pyramid.

I could turn around and just go back to my stupid summer vacation and wait for the time bomb to go off. I could just act like nothing had happened. But something *had* happened. And more would happen. It wasn't over.

I had rolled around in my bed last night feeling guilty that I didn't say something to Chaz. I let him drive off with a rattlesnake in the passenger seat. He never knew Janey was pregnant. He didn't know what Sharon was capable of. He was as helpless now as I had been when Animal was choking me to death.

I'd been mad at Chaz, but I couldn't stay mad. Chaz was my friend. He had saved my life. I couldn't leave him to an uncertain fate.

No, that was wrong. It was a *certain* fate. Some day Sharon would use her sister's diary. Some day she would turn on Chaz and then she would turn on me. It was in her nature to destroy.

Dad said that who we are is the result of decisions we made in the past. I suddenly understood that who we will become is the result of decisions we make in the present.

I drew in a deep breath and started up the stairs.

THE END

14650070R00119

Made in the USA
Lexington, KY
11 April 2012